CARNELIAN DOOR

VIRGINIA M. SCOTT

Publishing Partners

BOOKS BY VIRGINIA M. SCOTT

Palace of the Princess

Belonging

Balancing Act

Finding Abby

Don't Cross Your Heart, Katie Krieg

The Carnelian Door

Publishing Partners
Port Townsend, WA 98368
www.publishing-partners.com

Copyright 2017 © H William Brelje

LCCN: 2017938884
ISBN: 978-1-944887-20-9
eISBN: 978-1-944887-22-3

Cover Design: Marcia Breece
Typographer: Marcia Breece

DEDICATION

In loving memory of my mother and my mother-in-law.

ACKNOWLEDGMENTS

I would like to thank my father, Dr. C.E. Muhleman, for telling me great stories about the discovery of Tutankhamun's tomb during his boyhood, and for seeing a portion of those treasures with me much later in Chicago.

Thanks also to Don, Mohammed, Farouk and the rest who showed me Egypt; and to my best friend, Bill, who felt its enchantment along with me.

I am also indebted to novelist Phyllis A. Whitney, friend, and inspiration, who encouraged me to write *THE CARNELIAN DOOR*.

PROLOGUE

Upper Egypt
Necropolis of Thebes
18th Dynasty

Wageta breathed a sigh of satisfaction and deep peace as she secreted the great jeweled collar of her Queen in a hewn chamber on the west bank of the Nile.

As she looked one last time at the necklace's many rows of carnelian and lapis-lazuli interconnected with heavy gold, she remembered vividly her Queen wearing it as she had regally entered Karnak with great fanfare on the barque for the jubilee of her father, Tuthmosis I. How grand those days were! Now, however, winds of change were upon the land, and Wageta did not want her Queen's name to be defiled.

Keeping the collar intact was one last thing Wageta could do for her glory.

CHAPTER ONE

From the balcony of my room at the Mena House, the Great Pyramid of Cheops loomed mysteriously only a stone's throw away, daring my mind not to boggle as it contemplated the massive proof of the intricacies of an engineering feat over four thousand years old. I'd taken in the view and rhapsodized about my dream trip only hours before, in fact, as I'd written postcards with the Pyramids of Giza on one side.

Now, however, for the first time since my arrival in Egypt, the panorama failed to hold my attention. More immediately compelling was the photograph that burned my hand as I scrutinized it for the fourth or fifth time.

How odd to think that had not my niece been recuperating at home from chicken pox, I wouldn't even be holding the little square bombshell. On impulse and paying too much, thinking I'd mail the snapshot to five-year-old Tracy to cheer her up, I had let an Egyptian pose me atop a camel that morning. Tracy would love it—and probably laugh herself silly at the sight of Aunt Alyssa hanging onto the unexpectedly tall beast for dear life. In contrast to its rider's seriousness, the camel seemed to be smiling.

It wasn't actually a very good picture, which allowed me a little leeway to wonder if my eyes were playing tricks on me. Yes, there I was on my dromedary. Even with a brimmed hat shielding my head from the sun, black curls that were the bane of my existence spilled out haphazardly. My five-foot frame was distinctively petite even on a camel. The low building behind me was nondescript, but my eyes zeroed in on the group outlined against it, for there in the background, mixed in with several camel tenders in traditional robes, was a slightly blurred, but nevertheless arresting, figure that shouldn't be there.

Jeffrey. The erect stance was his, as was the casual but put together look of his short-sleeved safari jacket and bwana hat. He'd always worn his clothes like a model and had the dark good looks to pull it off, just as the figure staring back at me did.

The last time I'd seen Jeffrey was a little less than a year ago at Sea-Tac when I had driven him from our condo in the Seattle suburb of Bellevue to catch the first leg of his journey to Istanbul. A travel writer, Jeffrey was then updating a guidebook on Turkey. As fervently as I disliked seeing my husband of only seven months leave for three weeks, I recognized that it was part of his job, just as staying home this time was part of mine.

Or was it? Jeffrey hadn't thought so. We had bickered about my going on the trip—words that as things turned out would haunt me mercilessly.

I looked at the picture of the man who looked so much like Jeffrey, and the memory of our leave taking blossomed like an ink stain from deep within me.

"I wish you were going along," he had commented in a by-then familiar refrain as we waited in the airport lounge for his flight.

"Oh, so do I," I told him, hoping that my loving tone might stave off a last-ditch effort in Jeffrey's campaign to get me to go with him. Sea-Tac airport shortly before he was ready to depart for another continent was hardly the place or time to rehash the issue. Wanting to help him focus upon our reunion instead of the separation, I stroked his forearm tenderly as I leaned closer and added, "I have quite a homecoming in the planning."

But he wasn't giving up even at this eleventh hour.

"You could catch a later flight," he suggested. When I didn't comment, he shook his head and continued with, "I still can't believe you wouldn't jump at the chance to see Turkey."

That wasn't the point, darn it! Had I been free to go, of course I would have jumped at the chance. Not only did I, as a bride, find being separated from my husband almost painful, but I enjoyed traveling. Although Egypt headed my wish list, like most people I knew, I also wanted to see as many other parts of the world as I could. The Bosporus, the Blue Mosque and other Turkish attractions weren't too far down on my list of hopefuls. Even so, the plans for the trip had come up so recently that there was no way I could go.

"You know I want to," I reminded him, hoping that would be the end of it.

No such luck. Screwing his even-featured face into a stubborn look, he returned, "But you could, Lissa. You don't even have to work."

That was a moot point. Although it was probably true that financially I didn't have to work, I loved my job as a fifth-grade teacher and wasn't ready to give it up. I certainly couldn't leave my school high and dry by suddenly taking off for the Middle East in the middle of a semester, and I didn't really understand Jeffrey's persistence. Flattered at first that he wanted me along, I had gradually begun to feel that he had gone beyond sentiment, almost as if my going had become a . . . battle of wills, perhaps.

His attitude surprised me, because when Jeffrey and I had talked about our careers before we were married, he had supported my desire to keep working for at least a few more years, seeming to understand, respect, and even admire my feelings about teaching. "Your commitment to your profession won't make you any less dedicated to our marriage," he had assured me. We agreed that I could always go on the trips scheduled in the summertime or during school vacations, and we *had* combined a marvelous honeymoon in Greece with his work. Recently, though, he seemed to have forgotten that teaching wasn't just a job to me, and an unwelcome feeling or irritation prickled as I tried to formulate a reply that would gently close this matter once and for all.

Maybe my eyes flashed a cautionary message. Before I could comment, the knit of his brows eased as he said in a softer tone, "Hon, I know I'm terrible for pressuring you. Don't take me wrong. I just like to be with you every moment I can."

The emotion mirrored in the inky eyes behind his horn-rimmed glasses did it every time. Jeffrey was irresistible when they sparkled with such intensity. Feeling my irritation ebb, I placed my left hand over his and felt a current of exhilaration as I saw our matching wedding bands glisten richly under the artificial light.

"I understand," I told him, believing I really did. Then because I wanted our parting to be on a distinctly positive note, in a lighter vein I asked, "I miss you so much that when you're away, do you know what I do?"

"Tell me," he coaxed in the same playful mood, much

to my relief. "I sleep on your side of the bed."

Grinning, he said, "You've never told me that. Do you really?"

"I do, Mr. Rohrer."

"Well, Mrs. Rohrer, I shall return to that side of our bed in just three weeks." I still thrilled to be called Mrs. Rohrer. Little did I know that soon I'd be Lissa McKinnon again.

Just as I told him I loved him, his flight was called for boarding.

Since they were calling by rows, we had the chance to hug, then hug again, and to steal a chaste airport kiss. My final glimpse of him was as he looked back one last time before he turned and blew me one last kiss.

Jeffrey called twice from Turkey to let me know that his work was moving along well. Then one afternoon just four days before he was to return, after I'd spent the weekend at my friend Tara's house on Whidbey Island, I returned to Bellevue to find a message from our friend Steve Matson on the answering machine.

Brief and to the point, Steve's recorded voice merely asked me to call him as soon as I got home, adding that it was important. When I phoned him, he insisted that he come right over, but still wouldn't elaborate, and I grew increasingly uneasy as I waited for him to arrive. Since I knew it would take him at least half an hour to reach Bellevue, I made a pot of coffee and grabbed a quick snack of cheese and crackers for myself while the coffee perked.

Steve and I had met as students at Sammamish High School eleven years before and had hit it off immediately because of our mutual fascination for things Egyptian, which we'd discovered when we both chanced to go to a costume party as Egyptians. As it turned out, Steve's aunt had been to Egypt several times and had a vast collection of papyrus, lapis lazuli and carnelian jewelry, stone temple cats, and other beautiful objects. As I would learn in years to come, these weren't your usual souvenirs.

Some, in fact, were such skillfully crafted reproductions of ancient treasures that probably only an expert could tell them from genuine artifacts.

Steve's fascination for Egypt had taken root and flowered over the years as his aunt communicated her enthusiasm to the growing boy. I'm not sure what sparked mine, but the flame burned brighter after I had viewed the magnificent treasures from Tutankhamun's tomb when the touring exhibit was in Seattle. After that, of course I had burned to become an Egyptologist. When I found later, though, that teaching stoked a different kind of fire within me, I became content to let the study of Egypt remain an avocation. Even so, I had never lost the desire to see the land of the ancient pharaohs for myself.

When I majored in education at the University of Washington, he opted for art history at the University of Chicago; I became an elementary school teacher, and he returned to the Pacific Northwest as assistant professor.

Steve met Jeffrey Rohrer before I did, through their mutual interest in golf, which led them to the discovery that they both also appreciated ancient cultures and enjoyed discussing, for instance, parallel historical developments in Egypt and Greece.

Steve introduced Jeffrey and me, and the rest, as they say, is history. I was taken by Jeffrey immediately. Suave and darkly handsome, he radiated a certain something that had bowled me over almost from the first glance.

The peal of the condo's doorbell broke into my thoughts.

The first thing I noticed when I opened the door was that Steve looked terrible, and I immediately thought of the day many years ago when his beloved Irish setter had been hit by a car. Steve looked even worse now. An uncharacteristic hint of stubble forested his lower face, his hazel eyes were dull, and his entire body drooped.

What in the world? Could one of his parents have died? Since I cared for Steve and also knew and liked his family, I hoped his news would not be that dire.

"Come in Steve," I told him as he absently pecked me on the cheek.

It was our longstanding custom to talk over coffee or tea, no matter what, so I think I asked him to sit down while I poured him a cup of coffee.

As I turned to walk toward the kitchen, however, he took my arm gently and said as he motioned toward the couch, "No, Lissa, just come and sit down beside me. I have some bad news."

I was conscious as I sat down of Steve running his fingers through his wheat-colored hair, a gesture that made me shiver involuntarily because he did it only when he was very upset.

"What's wrong?" I asked.

In reply, he took my hands in his, and my life shattered as I heard him telling me that Jeffrey, the victim of a car-train accident, had died in Turkey. When I couldn't be reached, someone had contacted Steve.

Time stopped for several frozen minutes while, struck as mute as an ice sculpture. I absorbed the terrible message. Even then, a part of me denied it. I told Steve that there had to be some mistake. Jeffrey, though five years older than Steve and I, was, after all, only thirty-two years old.

Steve's right hand moved through his hair again before

he reclasped mine as he looked into my eyes. Did he see my world collapsing? Did he feel the coldness creeping from the pit of my stomach to every corner of my body? Did he sense the silent scream that threatened to erupt?

Not Jeffrey! my whole being insisted.

I vaguely remember prattling on, close to hysteria, about a mistake, but Steve pulled me back to reality by saying, "Oh, Lissa, how I wish we could leave it open to that possibility—to believe Jeffrey isn't gone—but they gave such a complete description, even mentioning the inscribed watch and the maple leaf birthmark behind one knee."

More than anything else, mention of the strange birthmark brought home the fact that it was not a mistake, and as seizure-like sobs shook me out of my icy stillness, Steve held me and patted my back.

Numbed, I sleepwalked through the next several days. My brother, Rob, flew up from Portland with his wife, and they, along with Steve and a few other close friends, were great support.

Jeffrey had no close family of his own, and we ended up having a simple but tasteful memorial service. Partly because his body had already been "taken care of" (I didn't ask for details at the time but learned at some point that it had been "aesthetically damaged") in Turkey, there was no actual funeral. Still, I might have tried to bring my husband home had not it been for Jeffrey's own words one day when death had still seemed eons away: "When I die, bury me in an unmarked grave. Just remember me well, and that will be my monument."

The strange rise and fall of the muezzin calling faithful Muslims to prayer snapped me back to the present.

In my room at the Mena House, I looked at the snapshot once again.

From the background, the man in the safari jacket, who looked more like Jeffrey than ever, seemed to be staring at my back as I sat on my camel, and for just an instant he and the camel tenders in their flowing galabias seemed to be part of a surrealistic frieze.

CHAPTER TWO

Since this was Egypt and I didn't intend to waste my time brooding, I resolved to put the photograph with the Jeffrey look-alike out of my mind, at least for now. After a light lunch at the hotel, I was eager to embrace the role of tourist again. There was so much to see!

On my first full day in Egypt, I had headed straight for that place of places, the Egyptian Museum, which I knew I would want to revisit at some point before I left for home. A single trip there cannot do it justice. From stone sarcophagi and wooden mummy cases to papyrus rich with hieroglyphic texts and ancient pictorial stories, from colossal statues to tiny amulets, and from modest household items to the blazing gold treasures of boy-king "Tut," the rooms offer an unparalleled, glorious walk through the millenia of Egyptian history.

Except for the museum, however, so far I had taken in more of the Giza area, including a close-up view of the pyramids and the Sphinx, than of Cairo proper, since my hotel was across the Nile from Cairo, in Giza. It was time to see more of Cairo, and I knew just where I wanted to start.

Several times a day, the muezzin's call to prayer permeated the air, lending a distinctly Eastern flavor to the metropolis. It also served as a continual reminder to me not to ignore the Islamic heritage of the vast majority of the current Egyptian people as I exposed myself to elements of Egypt's more fabled pharaonic past. With that in mind, I decided to make my destination the Citadel of Cairo, whose impressive walled bulk I had noticed on my taxi ride to Giza from the airport.

It was that wild dash through Cairo the evening of my arrival that convinced me not to rent a car for my own use, as I might have done elsewhere. In a city of millions, people milled everywhere, including in the roadways as they tried, sometimes literally risking their lives, to dart across a steady stream of traffic with a dearth of such pedestrian safety staples as cross-walks and walk/wait signals. At only a few of the busiest intersections—and "busiest" is relative since they all seemed congested to me—were there even stoplights to occasionally halt cross traffic for pedestrians. Brave beings wishing to cross the street dodged moving traffic in a strange dance that since I hadn't seen any bodies littering the streets, must have had a cadence of its own that Cairoans heard with an inner ear.

As for traffic itself, without dividing lines to indicate most driving lanes, vehicles and numerous donkeys, often in tandem with garlic-laden carts, moved along in ill-defined, frequently shifting lines that reminded me of Chinese dragons vying for space in the same parade. Their "snorts were the cacophony of countless blaring horns and occasional human epithets. What in America might be three lanes somehow managed to transmogrify to four, or even five, breadths of traffic in Cairo. If there was method to this madness, I wasn't privy to its secrets. I would leave the driving to others.

I changed from my camel riding outfit of khaki slacks and a shirt to a casual navy skirt, red-white-and-blue plaid blouse, and a pair of comfy walking shoes. I had bought a touristy canvas tote bag with the hieroglyphic alphabet on it, and into this I dropped items including a cardigan, my well-worn *Baedecker's Egypt* and, of course, packets of facial tissue. Since most bathrooms at tourist stops also lacked soap and towels, I also carried pre-moistened towelettes.

I was asking one of the hotel's pleasant desk clerks—Mervat, according to her name tag—the best way to get to the Citadel when a voice behind me said, "I will drive you." As it was with many Egyptians, his English was excellent, and for the umpteenth time I felt that we Americans might be missing the boat by not encouraging our young school children to become bilingual.

As I turned around, I saw that he was around thirty and smiling. He had a cigarette in one hand and wore chinos and a cotton shirt that strained over a slightly protuberant belly. A pack of American cigarettes made the shirt pocket bulge. He probably meant well, but I wasn't inclined to get into a car with a total stranger in a foreign land and declined as politely as I could.

"Hello, Asmie," Mervat greeted from behind her desk.

He also hailed her by name and then said to me, "Let me show you some of my city on the way to the Citadel."

And that seemed to be that with Asmie, who apparently assuming I would obediently follow, turned, and began walking toward the lobby doors. When he realized I wasn't tagging along, he shrugged his shoulders, smiled winningly and gestured for me to come.

My eyes met Mervat's, who told me with a musical laugh, "Asmie is pushy but is all right, Miss McKinnon. He runs a small shop here. You will be safe with him."

Hmmm . . . it was tempting, but hotel shop or not, the man was still a stranger. Just as I was about to turn down the offer more firmly, to my utter surprise the endorsement in Mervat's eyes won me over. I did almost back out when I saw Asmie's rattletrap car, but what's a ding, I decided, or twenty. I got in beside him.

As it happened, when Asmie told me he would show me some of his city, he had meant Giza instead of Cairo, and at first, especially since the man had grown uncommunicative as the ride progressed, I was disgruntled. Then I quickly became fascinated by a Giza off the beaten tourist path which bore scant resemblance to the rarefied atmosphere of my hotel or the allure of the pyramids. This was real Egyptian life, I realized. Although the people along the route looked content enough as they went about their daily business, the signs of poverty touched and sobered me. I did not see anyone who looked desperate for food, but at one point along a drainage canal, I saw people washing clothes in the same stagnant water where garbage floated, and I could only hope that the women filling jugs with the dirty liquid were not planning to use it for drinking or cooking. The multi-family dwellings they called home were of poor quality bricks and mortar, and were several years old but often half-finished, it seemed, with people living in some units, while the uncompleted portions, open to the onlooker like a dollhouse's empty rooms, had quickly become ramshackle. Other buildings were in various stages of decay.

As Asmie took me down the side streets of Giza, little open-air markets, obviously for locals and not the tourist trade, popped up along the way. One featured slabs of raw meat hanging from hooks in the warm air, and another, popular judging by its number of customers, specialized in whole fish.

Since it had not rained for a long while, the slightest breeze, including that generated by our passing car, blew dust onto the people, the meat and the fish. No one seemed to care.

Although in other sections of the Cairo metropolitan area I had seen many Egyptians in western dress, this neighborhood's mode of attire was entirely traditional, with men in galabias and women and little girls wearing long dresses and scarves to cover their heads. I stole another glance at Asmie's western clothing and wondered if this was his neighborhood.

"Do you live in Giza, Asmie?" I asked.

He nodded and said, "Over closer to the street that goes to your hotel." He didn't seem to want to elaborate about his home life and changed the subject by asking, "Would you like to see the camel market?"

"Camel market?" I asked in surprise. I guess I had never stopped to consider that there were such places, and for the first time I wondered if people ate camel meat. "Is it like the markets where we saw the meat and fish?"

"Oh no," he said as he laughed good-naturedly, "the animals are alive. You will never see so many camels in one place again in your whole life."

As long as they weren't slabs of meat, I thought it might be an interesting experience.

"Yes, I would," I told my guide.

We rode a little farther, and after Asmie had parked the car in the street, we made our way across a dusty expanse of earth toward some low buildings that turned out to be stalls. The smell was rank, the sounds were entirely foreign as men shouted in Arabic to the accompaniment of camel snorts, and not another tourist was in sight for as far as my eyes could see.

"Off the beaten street," Asmie commented, mangling the idiom just a bit.

"That's for sure," I commented.

As we penetrated the vast yard, I lost count of the number of dull-tan beasts standing in clusters everywhere.

"My word!" I exclaimed as we rounded the corner of a stall and I saw a still larger congregation of the animals. "How many camels are there?"

He shrugged as he told me, "Hundreds." He seemed to be getting a kick out of my new experience.

A group of robed men playing cards in the shade of one of the stalls eyed us as we passed, and when Asmie told them something in Arabic, they nodded, smiled, and quickly returned to their game.

As we passed them, Asmie gestured ahead and said, "See those marks on the camels?" He was referring to painted symbols, such as red circles, on the rumps of many of the dromedaries.

I nodded and learned that the camels were graded as to age, health and other factors, which determined their price and future. One cluster of especially thin, old-looking camels looked destined for the glue factory, but most of them seemed spry and healthy.

Although, except around the pyramids, I had not seen many camels being used as transportation within the metropolitan area, I knew that they were still venerable ships of the desert and in great demand in this sere land where never too far away sand stretched every which way.

"Men come from all over to buy and sell," Asmie told me.

Just then, as I heard a muted thunder behind me, I felt a switch flick sharply across my behind.

"What in the—"

Asmie did not need to explain. I cut myself off as suddenly I recognized the thunder as a group of galloping camels rushing up behind us. We quickly sidestepped out of harm's way.

"Whew! They're fast," I remarked. "Are you okay?"

"Fine. It's certainly a busy place." *And dusty,* I thought, as I watched a layer of dirt settle over our shoes.

On our way back to the car, one of the card players disengaged himself from the group and walked over to us as he said something in Arabic to Asmie. The gesture was easier to read. He wanted his picture taken.

"Is it all right?" I asked Asmie.

"Yes," he told me, apparently giving the smiling man a go-ahead in his native language, "but he wishes you to be with him in the picture. I will get some camels in the background. It will be a good souvenir."

Asmie snapped two shots, and then the camel trader took one of Asmie and me standing side by side. When he handed the camera back to me, he stood there as if waiting for something.

"Am I supposed to pay him?" I asked.

Asmie only shrugged, so I gave the man a few piastres and was rewarded with a blazing smile that revealed yellowed teeth. All the men seemed to smoke, and perhaps the strong tea they drank also did little to keep their enamel white.

Asmie and I walked around the camel pens a bit more and soon left the strange scene behind. As the car entered a better section of Giza, I looked at my watch and commented that I should probably be getting to the Citadel.

"Just one more stop?" Asmie asked so engagingly that I could hardly refuse.

"Well . . . where?" I asked. Asmie had been a perfect gentleman, but I knew little about Muslim standards of morality—about the Egyptian male—and did not want to inadvertently invite anything. When he told me the destination was a jewelry store with excellent merchandise at good prices, I felt relieved.

I shouldn't have been, because that's how I found out what Asmie had had in mind all along. The tour of Giza's back streets, the camel market, and the offer to drive me to the Citadel—all had been a prelude to getting me over the threshold of this small store that Asmie just happened to own. Although except for the sapphire ring of my grandmother's I wasn't wearing expensive jewelry, he had apparently pegged me as a rich American, out to shop 'til she dropped, and we had barely walked through the entrance before a saleswoman (Asmie's wife or sister?) began pointing out a selection of scarabs, amulets and cartouches.

I did love jewelry and couldn't resist looking.

Perhaps my eyes registered a possible sale when they spied the cartouches. Asmie walked closer and dismissed the woman as he pulled out a tray from behind the display counter, picked up one of the elongated oval charms, and handed it to me as he said, "Feel how heavy it is. It is 18-karat gold."

About an inch-and-a-half long, it did have a hefty feel to it, and the workmanship was excellent. I could tell from the combination of the solar disc, sacred beetle and other hieroglyphs that this was a replica of the royal seal of Tutankhamun. I had seen the real thing at the Egyptian Museum and, years earlier, in Seattle. Such replicas of actual cartouches abounded in shops all over Egypt. Although in ancient times hieroglyphs with an oval around them—a cartouche—always signified only a royal name, contemporary offshoots bearing your name or mine in raised hieroglyphics soldered onto a golden oval were popular souvenirs.

"How much?" I asked, and when Asmie quoted a price in Egyptian pounds, I whipped out my small calculator that converted pounds into dollars. It came to a sum so low that I probably should have realized it was much too little for 18-karat gold of such weight, but I felt beholden to this man, as ridiculous as it seemed later, for having shown me the seamy side of Giza.

Although I would wait to buy any additional jewelry at a store whose name I had from Aunt Miriam as indisputably reputable, I made a snap decision to order one of Asmie's cartouches for my friend Tara. When he produced a card with our alphabet and each letter's corresponding hieroglyphic symbol, I learned that Tara's name would appear vertically on the finished pendant as a loaf, an eagle, a mouth, and another eagle. We agree that he would bring the finished piece of jewelry to the hotel the next day.

Asmie tried his best to sell me other gold items, as well as lavish necklaces and earrings of lapis and other gemstones, but I was so steadfast in my refusal to purchase anything but the one cartouche that he soon became resigned, if grumpily, to having wasted his time on a woman with tight purse strings. I was soon on my way to the Citadel.

The Citadel of Cairo, begun in 1176 A.D. by Saladin, loomed above me as Asmie dropped me off. Its massive walls and squat towers, said to be made from stones used from some of the smaller pyramids, certainly gave it the appearance of the fortress it had been. Crenellations and slits in the towers for archers lent a distinct medieval flavor.

Offsetting this bulk were the tall, slender minarets of Mohammed Ali Mosque, also called the Alabaster Mosque, crowning the Citadel. Even as I delighted in the picture perfect scene of the pencil-slim towers and the mosque's complementary Byzantine domes outlined against a cerulean sky, a shadow scudded across my thoughts as I visualized Turkey's Blue Mosque, which I had seen only in pictures.

Turkey . . . Jeffrey . . . pain. The three words were inextricably entwined for me, and as I made my way up the Citadel of Cairo's long incline, a welter of emotions assailed me as my resolution not to brood evaporated. I felt a sudden stab of guilt, in fact, for even being in Egypt in the middle of a school semester when I had not budged from my teaching duties a year ago to go abroad with my husband.

He'd tried so hard to get me to go with him. Had he had some premonition of death? Could I have saved Jeffrey just by going along, or would I, too, now be dead? "I should have gone with him," I had recited like a litany after he hadn't come home. "Stop blaming yourself," others, especially my brother, had counseled. But even when a psychologist whom I'd seen briefly had told me essentially the same thing, I had not been able to let it rest. It was taking time and finding answers I could live with that would do it, and it was all too easy when guilt reared its ugly head to forget that I was away from teaching now only because I had reached the point where I had too little of myself left to give in the classroom. That had not been true a year ago.

I had come to the Alabaster Mosque's tiled forecourt, where vaulted galleries overlooked an open square dominated by an ornate fountain where Muslims washed before entering their place of worship. Near its entrance, I stopped while an attendant tied paper booties over my shoes.

As I walked into the building, I was struck by the beautiful foreignness of the prayer hall, whose vast floor space was covered with well-worn, unmatched carpets where pews would be in a church. Tapestries adorned the walls, and dozens of glass globes hanging from the ceiling on long chains illuminated the inside of the mosque with a candle-like glow. When my eyes traveled upward and out to encompass the interior of the great Byzantine dome, I drew in my breath, for the intricately patterned dome shone with gilt that looked like solid gold, and its girdle of small stained glass windows looked every bit like chunks of topaz and ruby and sapphire set into the shining hemisphere.

The *minbar*, or pulpit, was elaborately decorated, and although no _iman_ was present, I could imagine the scene, with his assistants on the *dikka*, a platform supported on columns, so that the congregation could see and imitate his genuflections and other aspects of worship.

Aunt Miriam had told me about the "wishing arches," so I made my way over to a forest green and gold arched wooden structure to the side of the prayer hall and made a fervent wish as I walked beneath to let sleeping dogs lie and enjoy my trip.

On the way out of the mosque, I peeked into the side room that housed the tomb of Mohammed Ali, who died in 1849, and heard a tour guide telling a group that he had broken away from the Ottoman caliph to found the dynasty that ended with King Farouk in 1952.

Outside, I looked once again at the ablution fountain and at the exterior of El-Nasir Mosque, whose Persian style included unusual minarets and bulbous domes with faience ornamentation. I also looked for Joseph's Well, the means by which those within the fortress had once brought water up to the Citadel. I could see the square shaft and knew that about halfway down oxen on a platform had worked a wheel.

From the Citadel's outdoor courtyard, I had a panoramic view of Cairo, which sprawled almost to the horizon in a gray, minaret-and dome-studded expanse. In the distance, I saw the Pyramids of Giza looking almost like a mirage through the haze of the warm afternoon.

Mirage.

The word grabbed at something deep within me. Was it because my marriage to Jeffrey had been over so quickly that it sometimes seemed like only a mirage or dream? I knew that if I traveled a distance, I could touch the pyramids that looked right now like a mirage, but what of my marriage? What was there to touch? A memory here? A keepsake there? Will-o'-the-wisp. What was in my heart had had no great architect, and it had no massive stones to make it concrete.

As I sat on a bench, I drew the camel photo out of my purse, and as I looked at it once again, I felt absolutely alone in a city of millions.

When I checked my box near the front desk for messages upon my return to the Mena House, Mervat had been replaced by another clerk, who handed me a sealed envelope and a bulky package.

As I walked along the sidewalk that led to the newer part of the hotel, I balanced the package in the crook of one arm while I pulled out a single sheet of paper that read: "Mrs. Miriam Matson requests that you bring the package home for her as a surprise gift for her nephew."

Mrs. Miriam Matson was Steve's aunt, and the gift was for him. I wondered what it could be. For its size, the item wrapped in gay red and blue paper was quite heavy. Since it wasn't sealed, I decided that looking wouldn't be terrible of me, but I would not chance dropping it by juggling it, my purse, and my tote bag as I walked.

After returning to my room, I placed the package on the bed and carefully pulled away the several thicknesses of protective paper.

How charming. It was a blue stone statuette of Bastet, the cat-goddess, looking quite regal as she sat ramrod straight. The haughty pose brought a smile to my lips.

"Steve will adore you," I told the six-inch high figure as if it could hear me.

Had I known how the stone cat was to complicate my life, I'm quite sure that I would have buried it somewhere in the abundance of sand that stretched past the pyramids, seemingly forever, into the Western Desert.

CHAPTER THREE

"Aunt Miriam would be delighted if she could see us sitting here together in the shadow of the pyramids," Steve Matson said as we breakfasted in the hotel's poolside cafe, the Oasis, the following morning. From our vantage point across a pool empty in the morning coolness, the Islamic Arabesque architecture of the old part of the Mena House, along with some eucalyptus trees, partially obscured our view of the desert monuments, but we could see just enough to leave no doubt that we were in Giza.

We had come to Egypt separately—Steve on business and I on a vacation—but we were not there at the same time entirely by coincidence.

After that emotional time when Steve had broken the news of Jeffrey's death to me, we had kept in touch, although I moved from Bellevue to Oregon to try to make a fresh start. That had taken some doing. Never a nervous person by nature, apparently I experienced a delayed reaction to the stress surrounding Jeffrey's untimely passing. Like a snowball gaining momentum and becoming ever larger as it rolls downhill, my nightmares and feelings of guilt and anger built, not diminished, as time went on. Fortunately, I saw the crisis building and was able to set up a leave from my teaching position before becoming ineffective.

It was my sister-in-law who suggested that getting away might be refreshing. Mightn't it be the ideal time to take that vacation in Egypt? She was right. Just planning the trip had been therapeutic.

Of course when Steve and I learned of each other's plans, we decided to overlap our stays in the land we'd both held in such high esteem from the time of our respective childhoods.

Looking at him now, I followed his gaze out toward the famous triangular shapes of great honey-colored blocks, where the Great Pyramid dominated the scene. There was an almost palpable aura, so that one could envision the procession of the thousands who were said to have worked on its construction, smell their sweat, and feel their aching muscles as they built for all eternity.

"I wonder how many pairs of eyes have been awestruck by the sheer weight of the ages," I commented. "And you're right. Aunt Miriam would be thrilled to see us here. After all, 'Where else in the world can you see one of the seven wonders of the ancient world and hear the muezzin's call to prayer at the same time?'" I said, quoting his aunt as we chuckled at the favorite statement she had practically run into the ground. We loved her for it.

"Where else indeed?" Steve returned as he took a sip of coffee that was too strong for my taste. Our light meal included delicious raisin-studded rolls and juice.

"How is she doing," I asked, wary of hearing Steve's reply since the woman who had also become "Aunt Miriam" to me was undergoing a grueling regimen of chemotherapy.

"Beautifully, Lissa. I'm sure that if a positive attitude can beat cancer, she'll manage to heal herself, though we're all relieved that she happens to have a great team of doctors in her corner."

"How I hope. Did you know that she sent me a bon voyage note, complete with list of must-sees, before I left? What a time to think of others."

"And so like her," he said. His admiration of the woman who had kindled his lifelong love of Egypt never failed to touch me. I knew he would treasure the Bastet, which sat snugly inside the tote bag at my feet.

A sparrow landed just then on the back of an empty chair at our table. Although maybe it wasn't the thing to do—Jeffrey certainly wouldn't have approved—Steve and I simultaneously offered it a bit of roll. Then we sat watching our feathered friend for a couple of minutes.

After it had carried away the second of its prizes, Steve looked from the bird to me and asked, "So, Lissa, how are you doing?"

I'm fine, Steve, except that I think I saw Jeffrey near the Sphinx. I may even have him on film.

Had I really entertained the notion that the man might be Jeffrey? Now that I thought about it again with a friend at my side, the idea seemed absurd. Whatever it was about it, though, instead of mailing the snapshot to my niece, I still had it tucked into a zipper compartment of my purse. Eyes drawn repeatedly to the background where the man not wearing the galabia stood, I'd found myself poring over the touristy photo in spite of myself. The harder I stared, the more the perfect nose and well-shaped lips had looked like Jeffrey's. Since the man couldn't be Jeffrey, however, no matter how closely he resembled my late husband, I saw no point in saying anything to Steve. This was our time to enjoy Egypt.

"Relaxing more by the minute," I told him, realizing that I actually was. Enthusiastically, I told him about what I had already seen and done. Then in the easy way old friends do, we talked about our families, mutual friends and jobs, which brought us to the topic of Steve's business in Egypt.

"How are you coming with the project you outlined on the phone?" I asked.

"The portals?" he asked as eagerness suffused his face. I thought how boyish my towheaded friend looked just then, especially since the sprinkling of freckles across his nose had darkened under the Egyptian sun to further the element of youth.

When I nodded, he launched into a narrative about his sketches of the doorways of Egypt. Steve had done a similar series, published in a book, on the entrances to the Gothic cathedrals of Europe, and now he had another grant and leave-of-absence from his teaching duties to do the Egyptian series.

"I'm finding them amazingly varied, from the delicate traceried ones in places like Old Cairo, to the massive ones at Abu Simbel. But here," he said as he bent over to retrieve his black artist's folio, which he handed to me, "a picture is supposed to be worth a thousand words, so take a look for yourself."

Since I remembered a time when, teased by macho friends, Steve had been embarrassed about his artistic bent and had squirreled away most of his efforts, his openness now touched me. That feeling changed to awe as I worked my way through the stack of drawings and took in their exquisite detailing.

"They're absolutely beautiful, Steve," I told him with feeling just after looking at a page showing a wrought iron door whose filigrees had been painstakingly executed.

I saw what he meant by variety. The portals ranged from the ornamental to the stout kind that really meant business, in everything from wrought iron to bronze and wood. Two doors particularly caught my attention. One was fairly simple, with a large Coptic cross dominating it, but its cobalt color was striking. The other was red-tinted and ornate, with large-winged angels looking like heavenly sentinels.

Turning the sketches of the two bas-relief doors so that Steve could see them, I remarked, "These are unusual. Where did you find them?"

"In Cairo's necropolis," he told me, referring to the city's vast cemetery complex that included Christian and Muslim sections.

"They look almost too grand to be in a cemetery."

"I had the same impression at first, but if you walk through the City of the Dead, as it's called, you will notice that many of the structures are more carefully and lastingly built, not to mention richly ornamented, than the ones most Egyptians call home." After the route to the camel market, I could well believe it.

"Are these doors to mausoleums then?" I asked.

"No. They're to rooms for the living, to what I think of as mourning or remembrance rooms, where families can go to be near the actual resting places of their departed loved ones. They take flowers there in annual remembrance and on holidays, but what fascinates me, Lissa, is that they also take food to eat there, which is reminiscent of the way the ancient Egyptians placed food and drink on an offering table for the spirit of the deceased. Considered blessed, the food was then eaten."

"Mourning rooms," I repeated. "They sound like little chapels." The concept was intriguing, and I tried to imagine what they looked like.

"Why don't you come see for yourself? I'd be happy to show you around this afternoon, unless a cemetery would bring back painful memories."

I knew he meant Jeffrey. Appreciating Steve's sensitivity, I told him that I didn't think the necropolis would do that. And it probably wouldn't. I had been inside the burial chamber within the Pyramid of Cheops, after all, with no problem whatsoever, unless you want to count stale air and steep climbing.

Happy with our plans, we talked a bit more and decided to meet at a hotel on Cairo's Corniche el-Nil that afternoon following our respective late-morning appointments in different parts of the city.

Since I had never actually met him, I'm not sure when, or even exactly why, I first got the idea of looking up Richard Calvin, a professor at American University/Cairo, but I had written to Jeffrey's old college buddy and his response had been cordial.

I took the shuttle bus from the Mena House to the Egyptian Museum, just off Midan el-Tahrir, Cairo's Liberation Square, but this time I didn't enter the museum. I walked, instead, toward the heart of the square, which is the hub from which the city's main streets radiate.

It was an area of attractive high-rises that included the hotel where I would meet Steve later, and the people I saw scurrying here and there looked prosperous and were often dressed in western business suits. The camel market seemed far, far away.

From Midan el-Tahrir, the walk to American University was not long, but what a difference a few blocks can make.

Like a Janus mask the modernity and look of affluence fell away as I soon encountered people vending vegetables from carts in the streets and sidestepped puddles of urine and donkey droppings. Apartment buildings once again looked unkempt, and I noticed for the first time that most of them, although they had shutters, lacked glass windows. I was touched, though, when I noticed that no matter how poor the building, occupants of individual units had often attempted to personalize their little corner of the world by painting the shutters, woodwork and balcony area in bright, cheerful colors. Grass green was popular, as were salmon and coral shades. Television antennae were an interesting juxtaposition to age-old flowing desert robes hanging from clotheslines on poles extending from balcony railings.

I was pleased to see that the university itself, which I entered by way of a gate near the library, was modern. A welcoming committee of sorts greeted me. As I looked for the right building, I smiled in response to the friendliness of two turbaned men in galabias who had been on a scaffold painting trim and were now breaking for hot, strong tea out of glasses. I declined when they offered me some, but I appreciated their gesture.

Once I had located the right building, I ascended several flights of stairs and found Richard's name on a brass plaque on a door easily enough, but now that I stood on the threshold, I hesitated to knock, wondering once again just what I was doing there. I had a strong hunch it was more than a simple case of one American seeking out another far away from home. Admit it, I told myself, in the back of your mind you think Richard might supply some answers to questions you have about Jeffrey—answers that might make him more understandable, more real. Even as I stood there, I knew I was grasping at straws, for what could an old college chum know that I, as Jeffrey's wife, had not? Maybe I should just forget the meeting and phone Richard with my regrets.

Before I could knock or retreat, the bright green door to his office swung open, and a woman who was probably a secretary jumped slightly, obviously startled to find someone standing just beyond the door. We exchanged smiles.

"Ooh!" she exclaimed as I noticed her flawless sepia-toned skin and dark, expressive eyes. "I was just about to knock," I explained.

"You must be Mrs. Rohrer," she said good-naturedly, using the married name I had discarded. When I nodded, she continued with, "I'm Dr. Calvin's secretary. Why don't you step in and sit on one of the chairs near my desk? He should be with you shortly."

"I'll do that. Thank you."

"Have a wonderful time in Egypt."

"Thank you, I will."

Once inside, I noticed a computer near a desk that sported a pink phone. I hadn't even taken a seat on one of the office's utilitarian chairs, though, before the inner door opened and a man I assumed to be Richard Calvin ushered me into his rather spartan inner sanctum after only a cursory introduction. He took his chair behind a sturdy desk piled with books and papers, and I sat on the only other chair in the room.

"So you're Jeffrey's wife," he stated. His intense gaze was perhaps only curiosity, but it made me think of a scientist viewing something rather unexpected under a microscope. I wasn't sure if my periwinkle shirtwaist dress passed inspection, but I knew it set off my blue eyes and dark hair.

"Widow," I corrected, though the word still grated unfamiliarly. I could do my own assessing. Richard Calvin, who I knew was Jeffrey's age, looked ten years older, thanks mainly to his almost anorexic leanness and thinning hair. I'd seen pictures of him taken thirteen or fourteen years earlier, when he had been much heavier, and although he had not been as handsome as Jeffrey even as a younger man, he had at least looked healthy then.

"Widow," he repeated. "You're a teacher?"

"Fifth grade," I told him, "and I really like my work."

"Well, that's something we have in common. You probably know that I teach within a teacher-training program."

"Yes, I remember Jeffrey mentioning that. It must be stimulating, Dr. Calvin."

"Richard," he amended, and I wondered why I had been so formal. Except for Steve, perhaps I was simply accustomed to calling professors by their titles.

"Richard. Tell me about your program."

He gave me a thumbnail sketch of it as he lit a pipe, and then he launched into a sad tale of a very crowded nation, especially in the Cairo area, and not enough schools, teachers or educational materials to keep abreast of the ever-mushrooming numbers of children. To accommodate as many children as possible, school sessions were in shifts, he explained.

"That's certainly an argument for the best-trained teachers possible," I commented.

"Especially since your counterpart here has fifty to seventy children as opposed to . . . how many do you have in your class, Lissa?"

"Only twenty-four." I told him. Wended, trying to

imagine dealing with two to three times that number, "and they can be a handful."

"That isn't so true here. The numbers pose a problem, but the children, by and large, are well-behaved, rather regimented really, and do a lot of learning by memorization, without much time for questions and answers."

In contrast, mine never stopped asking questions!

We talked a bit more about teaching in the United States as compared to Egypt, and as the conversation wound down, I realized that we were skirting the topic of Jeffrey. Richard must have been thinking along similar lines.

"I was sorry to hear about Jeffrey. You know that we met in our sophomore year at the University of Oregon, don't you?" When I nodded, warmth flickered across his face as he began to describe their winning debates and fraternity pranks. Looking at the gaunt man before me, I found it rather hard to imagine the interaction.

"Jeffrey often talked about you, Richard, and I guess that's why I'm here."

"I'm glad you are. Being widowed so young must be very painful. I can see why meeting your late husband's friends might be comforting."

I hadn't thought of it as comfort, but had Richard hit the nail on the head? Maybe so, in the sense that understanding Jeffrey more thoroughly might lift the heavy mantle of heartache I still wore. And yet Richard Calvin wasn't supplying any answers. I'd already known of the fun-loving side of Jeffrey's nature, already known that with his mellifluous voice and physical presence and bright mind he was a mesmerizing speaker, and knew that people tended to like him.

"I suppose it is," I replied. "Jeffrey talked about the same debates and escapades you just did. You must have been a pretty mean debater yourself, or the arguments would have fallen flat."

"We made a great team."

So had Jeffrey and I.

"Jeffrey was expansive," I told him, "about a time more recent he enjoyed with you, Richard, when he stayed at your home here in Cairo about two years ago."

Richard Calvin frowned and puffed on his pipe.

When he didn't say anything and the ticking seconds left an unnatural void in our conversation, I asked, "Is there something wrong?"

"*Odd* may be a better description, Lissa."

"What do you mean?"

He looked at me penetratingly and set the pipe into the ashtray near his right hand.

"I don't know how to say this, and maybe I shouldn't say it, but the fact is that Jeffrey did not stay at my home. I saw him, but our old easy camaraderie was gone. You know, in the *can't go home again* way. We met for a drink and had dinner at his hotel and that was it. Although Jeffrey said he'd phone my office before he left the country, it was a call that never came."

I nodded. Friendships did change. That part I understood. The part about Jeffrey's not having stayed with Richard puzzled me, however, because I distinctly remembered Jeffrey's description of Richard's place and how glad he was not to have been holed up in a hotel room for a change, which he usually was when traveling on the job.

"I must have misunderstood," I said to myself as much as to Richard. "When Jeffrey talked about your wife and children and home life, it sounded as if he had been a guest in your home."

Richard put the heels of his hands against his desk and leaned forward.

"But that's impossible!"

"What is?"

"You see, Lissa, I have no wife or children."

CHAPTER FOUR

Despite the unsettling conversation with Richard, I determined not to let it spoil the afternoon with Steve. Out of many, a cemetery might seem like an odd attraction to visit in another land, but in addition to Steve's interest in the doors there, burial places and funeral practices tell much about life. We have only to behold the grave goods from Tutankhamun's tomb or to consider the complexities of the pyramids to have windows onto a past when body preservation and insurance for a good afterlife through the inclusion of material items with the mummy were of paramount importance. Indeed, humankind's fascination with these ancient practices and such grand resting places of the dead as the tombs in the Valley of the Kings feeds Egypt's tourist industry.

Her more recent burial customs and monuments do not garner the attention of a pyramid, but they also let us glimpse the fabric of a culture.

As Steve and I penetrated Cairo's modern necropolis, I commented, "I see why they call it the *City* of the Dead."

As far as the eye could see, small structures that were above-the-ground tombs and what Steve had called mourning rooms lined the twisting dirt pathways in a way that reminded me of tiny houses flanking city streets. It was very different from the kind of cemetery I knew, with orderly rows of stone or bronze markers and an occasional obelisk or mausoleum.

"I suppose it's a ghost town in more ways than one," Steve said, "since this whole area is inside an old Roman fortress built in the first century A.D. Although we can't see any Roman walls at this point, we are actually within what was the Roman fortress of Babylon. When we leave, we'll exit a different way than when we came in, and you'll see the walls and towers. Today, cemeteries, churches, and houses occupy an area that once garrisoned Roman legions."

I tried to imagine the soldiers, their horses, munitions stores, hospitals, water tanks—the whole thriving community—but they were only hazy images.

"It's strange to say," I remarked, "but I feel a closer bond to the ancient Egyptians in that very long ago past than to the more recent Romans, who somehow never really belonged here."

"I know what you mean. I can't feel too sorry for the banished Romans, either, because although they did much to better the world, Egypt lost her identity and was impoverished under Roman rule."

I remembered that that had come to an end when the Arabs conquered Egypt in the seventh century.

As we walked on, the distinctive tips on the crosses all around reminded me that we were in the Coptic part of the necropolis.

"What do you know about the Coptic religion?" I asked Steve. "Not a great deal, I'm embarrassed to say.

The Coptic Church is the native Egyptian Christian church. It's based upon the teachings of St. Mark, who is said to have brought Christianity to Egypt in the first century, though many ancient beliefs, such as in the cult of Isis, also exerted a strong influence upon Coptic Christianity. At some point, the Copts broke away from Rome. Christianity, in any case, spread rapidly throughout Egypt. In fact, many of the old temples were converted into monastic centers, including Deir el-Bahri in the Valley of the Kings, which I know you are planning to visit."

I nodded and said, "It sounds as if it was going pretty strong. What happened? The Arab Conquest?" I knew that the Copts of today comprised a mere ten percent or less of the Egyptian population.

"Yes, but the conversion to Islam was slow, and the Christian community didn't shrink to a minority until about the time of Saladin."

"So the Copts are really the descendants of pharaonic Egypt," I commented.

"Yes, but so, in a way, are the Muslims who have preserved traditions. A large percentage of them have intermingled blood. Anyway, the Copts are a pious people, very given to ceremony, with ritualistic chants and visits to tombs of martyrs on holy days, for example. A sense of the supernatural pervades, in miracles such as the appearance of the Holy Virgin, and in magic that includes belief in the power of amulets. Interwoven are many threads from Egypt's ancient past."

"And this," I said motioning to the right of the path to a black iron door in a peaked cement structure a little taller than I. "must be one of their tombs."

Steve nodded.

As we walked closer, I saw that the door was two to

three feet square and featured a prominent Coptic cross running most of its length and width. A small white plaque with an Arabic inscription on it was fastened above the door.

"It looks so much like the door to an old-fashioned iron stove," I remarked. "Is that where the body goes in?"

"That's right, and see those stairs just to the right of the vault?"

"Yes," I told him as I took in the gaudy mustard-colored door at the top of the short flight of stairs. "I didn't see this particular portal among your work."

With a smile, he replied, "It's one of the ugly ducklings, to be sure, but it leads to one of the mourning rooms we talked about." The room adjacent to the tomb was about the size of a single-car garage.

"Come, you'll see much finer examples of doors," he told me enthusiastically.

As we were about to walk on, however, a young mother with two waifs appeared and, in the universal gesture of a hand putting invisible food into her mouth, conveyed that she wanted money to feed the little ones. The pleading look in her eyes, which fastened upon mine and held beseechingly, had me digging into my purse for a few piastre notes, which she took with obvious gratitude. Although apparently needy, the trio did not look truly desperate, and rounding out their diet just a bit on this day gave me a sense of hope I don't think I would have felt had they looked swollen-bellied and doomed.

"Did I ever tell you that one of the things I like best about you is that you're an easy mark?" Steve commented as we passed the threesome. "It means you're compassionate."

"Look who's talking," I returned affectionately, thinking of the way Steve always bought pencils on street corners and donated change each time he spotted a store's coin box for the March of Dimes or Muscular Dystrophy Association. He also donated his time to a hospice on a strictly voluntary basis.

As we walked on, soon I began seeing portals as beautiful and elaborate as those from Steve's folio, and occasionally I even recognized one he had drawn. Some were flanked by modest columns or friezes with angels, and several had bas-relief surfaces in rich jewel-toned colors that one would never see in an American cemetery, whose colors tended to be subdued.

"What do they keep inside the rooms?" I asked.

"If you want to see what one is like inside, you can peek into the one coming up on our left," he told me, motioning a short way down the path.

Once there, we ascended a flight of five or six concrete steps and, with the help of a flashlight, peered through a grille to behold a hodgepodge of abandoned items that ranged from overturned chairs and a scarred bureau to nondescript wooden crates—all coated with a thick layer of dirt and withered leaves. This room had apparently fallen into disuse, and although perhaps it was silly of me to be moved by its air of abandonment, I did feel sorry somehow for those who rested within the adjacent tomb, for it seemed that no one prayed here any longer or remembered. The family line must have died out.

I wondered what sitting in one of the little rooms and remembering Jeffrey might have been like. I would have kept it clean and in perfect order, and I might have brought iced tea to sip while I recited Robert Browning from Jeffrey's favorite volume of poetry.

As it was, Jeffrey had not even a simple grave for me to visit.

Would I have put flowers there on his birthday and

Memorial Day? Would standing over the spot where his earthly remains lay have comforted me? Brought flashes of insight to help me understand? I would never know.

For the next half hour, we continued our journey, but even when we spotted one of "Steve's" doors, my heart was no longer in it, and my friend of so many years noticed.

"Out with it, Lissa," Steve blurted as we stood in front of a bronze door that I wasn't really seeing.

"Out with it?"

"Something's obviously come up since breakfast," he said. After trying to read my expression for a few moments, he asked, "What happened at American University?"

How like Steve to zero right in. Although my eyes had been taking in the City of the Dead and on one level my mind had been attuned to conversation with Steve, another part of it kept playing back over the encounter with Richard Calvin that morning.

Why had Jeffrey lied to me? The question had turned lunch at the Nile Hilton's pleasant courtyard cafe to cardboard, for all the taste it registered, dogged me from shop to shop in the Hilton's shopping arcade as I browsed halfheartedly before meeting Steve in the lobby, and it clamored for an answer even as I shared the afternoon with Steve.

"Ha! You know me so well. I never could compartmentalize very well, could I?"

"Not with me," he agreed. He reached out a hand to guide me toward a low stone wall opposite the bronze door as he said, "Come, let's sit here, and you can tell me all about it."

I positioned myself on the wall next to Steve and, not sure what to say, played with the folds of my skirt. Where did a dead husband fit into the adventure of finally seeing

Egypt firsthand with a dear friend? A part of me yearned to talk about my feelings. Wasn't I here in Egypt, after all, partly to put some old ghosts to bed and get on with the rest of my life? At the same time I sensed that talking might be a route to that, though, I also wanted to block out thoughts of Jeffrey and just enjoy the here and now.

I looked from the periwinkle dress fabric to Steve, whose caring hazel eyes reminded me that he was interested in far more than playing tour guide or simply having fun. Their gentle warmth encouraged me, and as I felt my reticence slip away, I described the encounter with Richard Calvin.

"Did Jeffrey ever mention the name to you?" I asked, although I could think of no particular reason why he would have.

"He may have. You have to remember that I didn't play as much golf with Jeffrey after you were married. Even then, we didn't talk much about our personal lives."

I hadn't known that.

"He didn't say anything about staying with Richard when he was in Cairo?"

"Not that I recall."

Then something occurred to me, and involuntarily my hand flew up to my mouth as I took in a swig of air.

"Lissa?" Steve asked. "Are you all right?"

"I just had a terrible thought. Steve, was there another woman?"

"I don't follow."

"Did Jeffrey have a . . . mistress?" I asked, for want of a better term. The idea of Jeffrey with another woman after he'd made a commitment to me further pulped my already bruised heart, but unfortunately the thought was there, and I had to consider the unpalatable idea.

"For your sake," he told me evenly, "I hope not, but the truth is, I just don't know. You know better than I that Jeffrey was attractive to the ladies."

That was certainly true. Although Jeffrey had never been openly flirtatious with other women in my presence, I had seen, with some amusement, many a female's interest perk up in response to his dropdead good looks. Mine certainly had, and I could feel myself blushing.

"We weren't married yet at the time of his trip, but . . . oh, I don't know," I said, holding up the palms of my hands in exasperation at not being able to find the right words.

"But you're jealous and hurt?" Steve finished for me.

I nodded. "I don't know about the jealous part, but mistress or none, I am hurt that he lied to me."

"Maybe it's time Jeffrey fell off his pedestal."

"What did you say?"

"I'm sorry, Lissa. If only you knew."

"What is that supposed to mean?"

"I'm not sure. Me and my big mouth."

I didn't say anything.

Steve continued with, "Don't be too hard on Jeffrey. It doesn't make it right, but you weren't married yet, and if there was another woman on that trip, Jeffrey was probably only trying to cover his tracks and spare you what he knew would be painful knowledge."

"Then why do it?"

"I can't answer that, Lissa, but it's what happens after the wedding that counts."

Of all the stupid things to say! I knew Steve was right, in a way. It *was* what happened after the wedding that mattered, but he seemed to be brushing away my hurt as inconsequential. How could he sit there and defend a man's broken commitment?

I slid off the wall and faced Steve as I said, "So now you're defending Jeffrey?"

"Lissa, Lissa, come back here," he said as he patted the wall. "Defending him? No, not really, but look at it this way. Jeffrey is gone. We can't know what was going on in his mind or be sure why he didn't tell you the truth. Haven't you tormented yourself enough? Even without this latest thing with Richard Calhoun—"

"Calvin," I corrected as I sat back down.

"Calvin. Even without this, you think about Jeffrey almost all the time, don't you? You look so sad sometimes. Look, I didn't mean to make it worse. Maybe it's this place. I shouldn't have brought you here."

Was I that transparent? In spite of my resolve not to let my inner turmoil show, I'm sure I did openly wear my emotions, including sadness, sometimes. *Sad*. What a word. Yes, I was sad, but not for the reason Steve probably assumed. How could I ever explain even to Steve, with whom I had shared so many thoughts over the years, that what had just about hamstrung me emotionally wasn't as simple—if death is ever simple for those left behind—as my husband's death? It went much deeper than sadness and was something I had shared with no one. I wasn't sure if I could with Steve.

"I wanted to come here, Steve. The problem is inside of me, not with the surroundings. I guess you've caught me in some unguarded moments."

I wasn't prepared for the combination of hurt and anger I saw cross Steve's face. Eyes closed, he shook his head slowly from side to side. Then they blinked open and impaled me as he said, "You know, Lissa, in the old days there were no unguarded moments."

In the old days . . . before Jeffrey.

Still seated on the wall, I looked at my hands for a long moment, and when I glanced at Steve, he was gazing, seemingly lost in thought, out over the cemetery grounds. Perhaps he was remembering our shared confidences of the past. Politics, sex, religion, broken hearts, and dreams; no topic had been taboo until Jeffrey had somehow changed the chemistry between us.

Feeling a rush of affection for my longtime friend, I let my left hand close around his right one, and the gesture pulled him back from wherever his thoughts had flown. He didn't respond to my touch but neither did he pull away his hand.

"Do you ever want it to be the way it used to be?" he asked so longingly that I was choked up.

"When you could tell me anything and I could tell you anything?

Very much," I told him softly, blinking away the salty mist that had filled my eyes.

Just as softly, he invited, "Why don't you try?"

I had been looking at the bronze door as we spoke. Now I turned my body so that, still sitting beside him, I faced Steve squarely as I said, "Steve, I wish I could. It's just . . . just that I think about Jeffrey at odd times, and when I do, well, I still hurt. I can't seem to verbalize it. I . . ."

Whatever I might have said stayed unvoiced. A tour group, noisy even in this subdued setting, effectively cut me off.

"German?" I asked Steve, who had a broader knowledge of languages than I.

"I think it's some Slavic tongue."

By the time they had passed, the intimacy of the moment was gone.

Perhaps waiting for a cue from me, Steve did not pursue

what we'd begun to discuss before the little knot of humanity walked by, and neither did I.

I wasn't even sure the words had been there yet.

Had I spoiled our afternoon? If so, maybe I could still salvage it.

"Come on," I said, hopping down from my perch, "let's go find one of Aunt Miriam's must-sees. The Church of Abu Sarga can't be too far from here."

Steve hesitated momentarily and then stood up as he said, "All right, but there's one condition to that."

"And what might that be?"

"That sometime we continue the talk we were having when the tour group happened by."

I didn't know when I would be ready, but Steve's invitation to pick up where we'd left off made me feel less alone, and suddenly the day seemed full of promise again.

"It's a deal," I told him.

The Coptic Church of Abu Sarga, of St. Sergius, was founded in the fourth or fifth century and rebuilt over a place where, as tradition has it, the Holy Family found refuge during their flight into Egypt.

Aunt Miriam had recounted her moving experience of having been in the subterranean chamber where Mary supposedly rested with the baby Jesus, and as we neared the church, I mentioned the crypt that had drawn pilgrims and tourists for centuries.

"Is it true, Steve, that the crypt is now inaccessible?" I asked.

The area had been flooded with the building of the Aswan High Dam, and I wasn't sure if efforts to keep it dry had been successful. Fortunately, Aunt Miriam had visited the crypt earlier.

"As far as I know it's still off limits," he told me with regret in his voice. "Heaven only knows the extent of the damage and destruction that dam has brought. At least Abu Simbel and Philae were saved."

"Thank goodness for that. That's *progress* for you, I guess," I said, thinking of the high price we sometimes paid for such bonuses as electricity.

"Don't get me started," he told me, rolling his eyes. I was relieved that we were back to being more like our old selves.

"Here we are," he added as we came to a flight of stairs leading down. "It's not the prettiest church in the world, but it's a perfect example of the Egyptian Byzantine basilica."

As we entered, I saw what he meant. Rather dark at this time of day, it had a nave and aisles, exposed beams, a raised transept, and galleries. Hanging from the ceiling were brass oil lamps which illuminated the church enough so that we could note traces of life-sized human figures that were probably apostles or saints on marble columns that separated the aisles from the nave. Above the row of columns was a band of keeled arches that, in turn, supported another row of columns.

As my eyes traveled down the length of the room, I saw a freestanding marble pulpit on columns. Beyond that was a wooden sanctuary screen, behind which only those in holy orders could go, thus preserving an element of mysticism. I imagined incense and chanting in the strange Coptic language that had been a direct communication with the past.

Although the church was empty of but a few other tourists, Steve and I felt a mutual urge to remain quiet as we observed icons, mosaics, and some eleventh century wooden panels that delighted the artist in Steve.

As we moved along our way into the side chapels, we saw iron bars blocking a rough stairway.

"That's where the crypt is, Lissa," Steve told me softly, "down those stairs."

I thought of the small vaulted chapel Aunt Miriam had described, with an altar marking the spot where the Holy Family had rested. A man was standing by the entrance now, peering futilely beyond, and as we watched him gently stroke a bar of the door, Steve and I exchanged glances, understanding the pilgrim's awe.

It was when we turned to make our way back out into the main part of the church that I saw a retreating figure that made me take a second look.

He was just an Egyptian in a rather old brown suit, and I probably would not have noticed him at all had not he looked vaguely familiar.

It was only later that I wished I'd gotten a better look at him.

CHAPTER FIVE

I n my hotel room that evening, the eyes of the proud-looking Bastet seemed to bore a hole into me as I sat in bed trying to get hooked on the romantic-suspense novel I had brought from home. Through no fault of the author, however, the main character's plight did not hold my attention.

I set the book onto the lamp table and walked across the room. "Trying to mesmerize me, are you?" I said as I picked up the statuette from its perch atop the television set and was struck again by its queenly bearing. It sat frozen forever in a sitting position, the base of the statue its throne.

Bastet—goddess of joy and love, guardian of the home. *Home*: such a warmth-eliciting word.

At first, I wouldn't have dreamed of leaving the condominium that Jeffrey and I had so happily chosen as our first home and furnished in an eclectic blend that merged our tastes and showed our appreciation of good pieces from many eras and cultures. There was the little rosewood escritoire that had been my grandmother's, the Chinese coffee table that Jeffrey had brought home from one of his trips before we were married, and the bleached mahogany bedroom suite that we had selected together.

It was a home redolent of his homemade cinnamon rolls on rainy Sunday mornings, a home alive with the strains of film soundtracks and Broadway show tunes as I graded papers and he polished articles, a home where we had made love more than once in front of the crackling living room fireplace.

And then suddenly it was all over. Jeffrey was nowhere—yet paradoxically everywhere—in our condo, so that our little nest, just by looking as it always had when he was alive, began to taunt me for trying in vain to keep everything the same.

First, there had been numbness, followed by grief that washed over me in nauseating waves. How could I survive without the man with whom I had been so sure I would spend the rest of my life? I didn't doubt my ability to earn a living or balance my checkbook or keep my car running smoothly, but who would build a future with me, be the father of my children, and grow old at my side?

In a thousand ways, I had yearned for Jeffrey, and the absence of little routine things—the countless ways of unmeshing—ripped at the core of my being. Reading the morning paper before work, for instance, tore me up, continually reminding me as it did of the way Jeffrey always went first for the stock market report, while I preferred the front section. A hard news junkie, Jeffrey had called me. We had worked out what we'd dubbed the Rohrer Newspaper Protocol, accommodating our tastes, and it had come to feel very natural. Similarly, because we had so often run together, jogging solo suddenly became a painful exercise as I remembered his panther-like grace.

Then, there had been guilt, the wondering if I had

put my teaching before my marriage. Time after time, I'd castigated myself for not having traveled with him, wondering if I'd gone on that trip to Turkey he might not have died.

As crushed as I initially was after Jeffrey's accident, I instinctively knew that getting back to work would be the best tonic, and that's why only three weeks after the terrible evening when Steve had broken the news of Jeffrey's death to me, I was back in the classroom.

In a strange way, my ten-year-olds lent a modicum of comfort that family and friends could not. My students didn't walk on eggshells or tell me I was young and would one day find another husband. They didn't tell me what to do, or what not to do. They were just there with their wonderfully inquisitive minds. In focusing upon them instead of on my loss—although I did dwell upon that in many lonely, aching hours—I had gotten through the school year before moving to Oregon.

The Bastet in my hand suddenly felt quite heavy. As I set it back down, my eyes fastened upon the hieroglyphic inscription chiseled into its base, and I realized that my left thumb was absently rubbing my naked ring finger. Even the ancient Egyptian writing brought back memories of Jeffrey, for we had had a goldsmith custom design our wedding bands with our names encircling them in raised hieroglyphs. "Something unique to celebrate our unique love," Jeffrey had said. Even here in Egypt I had not seen any like them.

Jeffrey's ring had not been with the personal effects returned to me. Mine, which had stayed securely on my finger for a time, was at home in a memento box in a far corner of my closet. Wishing it could have been more like a movie I had seen many years ago in which a young widow sings a song in an empty room and, oh so tenderly, removes the ring her husband had slid onto her finger on their wedding day, I had pulled it off in sadness tinged with hurt and anger.

The domino that began to topple all I held dear in my love for Jeffrey was the bill for his vasectomy, which I had found locked inside his desk several weeks after his death. Had the date of the surgery preceded our marriage, I could have coped more easily, for even though a vasectomy is a serious matter to hold back from a prospective wife, to some extent I could understand a man's reluctance to reveal his incapacity to biologically father a child. What was done was done. Jeffrey and I could have adopted.

He had had his operation after our wedding, though, only two months before his fatal trip, when he was supposedly on a business trip to San Francisco, and I was dumbfounded that he had not talked it over with me first. Especially in light of the fact that we had discussed having children and agreed that, God willing, we would have one or two somewhere along the line, how could he have just gone off on his own and taken a step that would so affect our future? Whatever reason he may have had to end his fertility, couldn't he at least have given me the chance to understand and support him in the decision? That I had grown to know his body like a well-worn road map and yet not guessed his intention or what had driven him to do this secret thing seemed incredible.

Another domino was the savings account passbook that I also found only after his death, with deposits far exceeding a travel writer's income. The money never stayed in the account for long, and it had been closed shortly before Jeffrey left for Turkey on that last trip. Citing confidentiality, the bank would tell me nothing since the account had been in Jeffrey's name alone.

And now there was another question left hanging. Another domino? Had Jeffrey been with a woman instead of with Richard Calvin in Cairo? Even now, with Jeffrey dead, the thought sent a stab of . . . yes, jealousy, despite my protestation to Steve, through me. I could handle whatever had happened to Jeffrey romantically before he met me, but to think that he may have sought out another woman, even for just a casual fling, after having made a commitment to me hurt like the dickens. "It's only us from now on, Hon," a Jeffrey still tousle-haired from our lovemaking had told me before leaving for Egypt only weeks before our wedding. I had believed him wholeheartedly.

Ours had always been an intensely physical relationship. From the moment we met, I was attracted to Jeffrey as I never had been attracted to a man previously. Before Jeffrey, there had been Michael, with whom I had grown more physically intimate than I'd been with anyone up to that point. Michael always asked if I found him attractive, and I always said I did, which was true, but the fact remained that I could take or leave the physical aspect of our friendship. For me, the best part of Michael had been our mutual affinity for vintage films and Szechuan food on Friday nights. Many of his interests paralleled mine, though apparently not in bed, and to Michael that was a vital shortcoming.

Then Jeffrey had entered my life like a tornado, and I knew immediately what had been missing with Michael.

It was funny, too, because I'd come so close to not meeting Jeffrey at all and happened to only as a fill-in date when the friend of Steve's then-girlfriend couldn't make it a foursome at a Seattle Supersonics basketball game. That left Steve with an extra ticket near the floor in midcourt. Would I like to meet his golfing buddy Jeffrey and see the Sonics play?

Would I! I was a confirmed basketball nut and a rabid Sonics fan.

On my teacher's salary, though, my budget didn't extend to pro ball tickets—and definitely not such choice seats—very often. So I went, and the Sonics played a close game that night, winning in overtime by only one point.

What I remember best about that night, however, is Jeffrey in his green turtleneck enthusiastically cheering the team on. His dark eyes sparkled, and his sensuous lips frequently curved into a melting smile as we exchanged glances. He was so vital, so alive. When the Sonics had clinched the cliffhanger and we hugged, perhaps we had sealed our fate.

Steve, who hadn't thought Jeffrey was my type as more than a fill-in date, was stunned that the two of us had hit it off so quickly.

Steve . . .

When my eyes strayed to the Bastet again, this time I thought of him and his aunt. How like her to devise a special surprise for the man who was unabashedly her favorite human being. Miriam Matson was actually Steve's great-aunt. Young even at the age of seventy-six, she had been the spryest septuagenarian imaginable until her cancer had curtailed her activities. Why, just since her seventieth birthday, she had taken her first hot air balloon ride and ridden on a sled behind a team of malamutes in Alaska.

In addition to her zest for life and fascination with things Egyptian, I had come to admire Miriam Matson's philosophy almost as much as Steve did.

"Except in a pinch, none of this 'one day at a time' malarkey for me," she had vowed. "Don't take me wrong, Lissa. We all live that way at some points in our lives. It's a marvelous, even necessary, way to get through bad periods and a great way to endure physical pain. It's also a sane approach to something like alcoholism. I just don't like it as a guiding force, because life is too wonderful a canvas to fill out disjointedly, square by square, without breadth of vision. To do more than merely exist, maybe we need some kind of dream, some goal or whatever you'd call it that spans more than a day."

And yet when Jeffrey had died, Aunt Miriam had been there saying this was a "pinch" and time to take life one day at a time.

Now with her cancer, Aunt Miriam, too, was making do in a pinch, one day at a time.

I picked up the Bastet again and carefully rewrapped it and replaced it inside my tote bag, patting the mound as I thought warmly of both the gift giver and the prospective recipient.

After our tour of the City of the Dead, Steve and I stopped at a restaurant where we had relaxed over Rubis d'Egypte, a dry rose wine, and a dinner of veal, vegetables and *ooshari*, a pasta and rice dish with lentil, onion and ginger sauce. We even split a delectable chocolate mousse with raspberry sauce. Since I hadn't been hungry on the heels of my appointment at American University, I'd barely eaten since morning and was famished.

I'm sure that thoughts of Jeffrey and, to a lesser extent, Richard Calvin lurked in the back of our minds, but their names did not come up and we enjoyed our easy conversation about our day, ourselves, and Egypt.

"That was a fascinating tour of the necropolis, Steve," I told him again as he dropped me off at the Mena House after dinner. "You make an excellent tour guide."

"Farouk Matson at your service, m'dear," he joshed with a mock bow.

"Farouk" and I, who had made plans for a full day of sightseeing the following day, set a time for the next morning's meeting and called it an early night.

Instead of walking to my part of the hotel after he dropped me off, I went to the older building to see if Asmie had dropped off my jewelry order. As I entered the mirror-and-wood ceilinged lobby, I looked off to my left toward a windowed bar and was treated to an illuminated Pyramid of Cheops looking close enough to touch. *One could,* I thought, *easily become thoroughly potted here, drunk on alcohol in combination with "that view,"* as I was coming to think of the pyramid I saw so often from my room.

There was a small package waiting for me, but a tour group had just returned to the hotel and was beginning to clog the lobby, so I took it back to my room. As I walked across the lawn, the sights, sounds, and smells of the camel market returned to me—an experience certainly *off the beaten street,* as Asmie had put it.

The moment I unwrapped the charm earmarked for my friend Tara, I knew I had been the victim of a classic bait-and-switch scheme, which perhaps served me right, come to think of it, for not having been more cautious. Like anyone else, though, I hated getting ripped off.

Hmmph! I thought as instead of a heavy gold cartouche like the sample Asmie had shown me in his shop, I found a very thin, inferior quality charm that just wouldn't do. At least I had paid for the personalized gift by credit card, so the last laugh would be mine. I would instruct the bank to stop payment and return the piece of easily bendable metal to Asmie at the earliest possible opportunity.

Feeling naive and stupid, I relaxed in a tub of water and then curled up with the novel that hadn't held my attention.

I was about ready to turn off the light and try sleeping

when the phone jarred the room's stillness.

"Hello," I answered, thinking it must be Steve.

"Lissa?" came a voice only vaguely familiar. "Richard. Richard Calvin."

"Oh, hello, Richard."

Our visit had fizzled out after neither of us seemed to know how to deal with the revelation that Jeffrey had not stayed with Richard, and I had not expected to hear from him again.

"I feel terrible for having upset you in my office today," he told me now. "How are you doing?"

"I'm fine," I said. "Don't worry about what happened. I must have had my facts mixed up." I didn't think I had, but there wasn't any point in making Richard feel like a clod.

"As long as there aren't any hard feelings."

"Of course not," I said even as I wondered again why Richard had cast that shadow of doubt my way. I supposed it could have just popped out. Whatever the case, a widow can do without the burden of hearing that her husband has lied.

"Would you be free for dinner with me tomorrow evening?" he asked.

"We could talk some more about education in Egypt."

"That would be lovely, and I'd like to, Richard, but actually I'll be out all day. A friend from the Pacific Northwest is here, and we plan to head out toward Memphis, making a day of it. Then I'll be off to Luxor for a few days."

There was a pause, and although I didn't hear anything, I pictured him puffing on his pipe.

"I understand," he told me. I thought I heard disappointment in his voice before he added, "Maybe when you get back. Give me a call if you have some free time."

"I'll do that," I told him, thinking that possibly we could talk over a drink, if nothing else. I didn't want to make any firm plans with him. Not only was Richard Calvin's tie to Jeffrey too strong to fit into a relaxing time, but I wasn't sure I liked the man.

As we rang off, I wondered again what Jeffrey had really done on that trip to Cairo shortly before we were married. He was ostensibly here to gather information on hotel accommodations for the disabled.

Had he ever written that article? I thought so, but in the excitement of becoming his bride so soon after his return, the topic had gone on one of my mental backburners, so that now I wasn't sure.

And yet if Jeffrey had been playing around, why would he have bothered to use Richard's name as an alibi and invent a family for him? Might not the old college chum sooner or later meet the wife and spill the beans? Whether or not Jeffrey had had a lover on that trip, though, there had been deception of some kind, just as there had been secrecy with the vasectomy.

It hurt like crazy and left me feeling very confused.

CHAPTER SIX

Braver than I, Steve rented a car for our day long excursion to Memphis, Egypt's once-splendid capital, and Saqqara, of Step Pyramid renown, and did an excellent job of maneuvering our borrowed Peugeot through the ubiquitous traffic, which mercifully thinned as we left the hustle and bustle of the Cairo/Giza area.

"The scenery will soon remind you of something out of biblical times," he told me.

As we rolled out of the city, we traveled not into the desert as I had expected, but through lush Nile-irrigated countryside on a two-lane road that followed an ancient canal. Soon I began seeing what Steve meant.

To my left, just across the canal, were green fields broken by stands of tall date palms. We passed men tending rows of young corn, not with tractor, not even with animal driven plow, but with crude hand implements that I instinctively knew had not changed much from the ones used by the farmers' distant ancestors. Donkeys abounded in the fields, on the road with riders on their sturdy backs or pulling carts heavily laden with crops, and in front of the meager dwellings made of mud bricks, palm and other natural materials. We recognized some of the people to the right of the roadway as bedouins from their black, head-to-toe attire. Even though I was in a motor vehicle with a man wearing contemporary khakis and a maize polo shirt, I had the sensation of having regressed in time by centuries.

Steve and I had fallen into a comfortable silence. Our eyes were so busy drinking in the verdant panoply of growing things and ancient images that we didn't need many words, although occasional scenes inspired our comments.

"Look!" I exclaimed at just such a time, pointing across the canal to a waist-high horizontal wheel about eight feet in diameter that was being powered by an ox as a child of around ten supervised. "I can't believe I'm seeing this so close to Cairo. Isn't that a water wheel?"

"A <u>saqiya</u>," Steve verified. "It's amazing, isn't it? We're probably only ten miles or so from a teeming metropolis. Doesn't the little girl remind you of a picture from one of your old Sunday school pamphlets?"

"She certainly does." With her bare feet, a dress that was timeless in its faded shapelessness, and a length of bright cloth over her head that trailed down her back Madonna style, she might indeed have leapt straight from a Bible story.

Soon the car passed the child, and Steve gestured toward an emerald field as he told me, "That's alfalfa."

"To feed all those donkeys," I remarked, thinking how much alike they all looked with their mottled gray and white coats and identical placid, rather bored looks on their faces.

"Memphis isn't much farther now."

As we turned off the main road, we passed through a quiet village that postdated Memphis, whose heyday had been during Egypt's Old Kingdom, and noted a few scattered stone remnants of the older city to the sides of the road as we made our way to a tourist stop. Accustomed to crowds at other Egyptian attractions, I was pleasantly surprised to find only one tour bus and three or four cars when we parked in the small lot.

Our first stop was an open-air building erected expressly to protect a colossal statue of Rameses II, the 19th Dynasty pharaoh who reigned for sixty-seven years. Information plaques told us that the limestone figure, excavated in 1820, once stood near the entrance to a temple. No less regal now, the likeness of Rameses II, his cartouche and stylized plaited beard proclaiming him Pharaoh, lay on its back. My eyes gravitated to his ears, which I'd read somewhere measured twenty inches in length.

Quietly, hand in hand, Steve and I inched our way along the statue's length and then ascended a stairway to a balcony so that we could look down upon the pharaoh's peaceful countenance from above. During his New Kingdom reign in the thirteenth century B.C., Rameses II had been responsible for a phenomenal amount of building, and since about half the existing temples dated back to his time, I knew I'd see ample evidence of his influence throughout Egypt. I wondered as I looked down at his statue if, as some say, he had also been the infamous pharaoh of "let my people go" repute.

A large tour group began crowding in, so we descended the stairs and walked back outside, where we drank in the clean, fresh air as we made our way toward an open area that featured several statues. One of these was an alabaster sphinx excavated in 1912. Tiny in comparison to the Giza Sphinx, it still weighed a hefty eighty tons.

As we sat on a bench near the Sphinx of Memphis, we enjoyed the contrast of the lion-man's whiteness to the brilliant green background of the vegetation as we felt a heavenly breeze ruffle our hair. The March sun was just comfortably warm, and I felt a sense of peace wash over me as I saw the way the graceful curve of the palm trees framed statues from the distant past. I closed my eyes to savor the feeling.

As I opened them, I said, "What a wonderful day to be alive."

"Definitely. I can tell you feel something special here, too, Lissa."

"I do," I replied. "With so little of Memphis left to see, it's strange to say, but I find this a peaceful, almost enchanted spot."

"So do I, and I can't quite put my finger on it. Maybe less is more. There's tantalizingly little left to suggest the grandeur of Memphis, that's for sure."

"Yet we know it existed."

"Exactly, and for those with imagination it almost still does."

Then he looked from the scenery to me and said, "This may sound odd since this is Egypt and those are palm trees growing in the wild, but it reminds me of our grove."

Steve was referring to our afternoon in an Oregon filbert grove last fall. The trees there had been planted so symmetrically that one could look from any point within the grove down distinct "avenues" separating the precise rows of filberts. It was a clean-smelling, quiet place just off a subdivision of modest homes, and that afternoon a young cat that seemed as playful and elusive as a wood sprite followed us as, enjoying the natural beauty and each other as we talked about all kinds of things, we had walked up and down the wooded avenues. Not a sound had broken the stillness, and we might have been on an island of our own.

"It doesn't sound odd," I told Steve now. "This spot has that same element of . . . oh I don't know . . . perfection."

We continued to admire the tranquil beauty of the scene until the tour group spilled outside. By mutual consent, we began walking back toward the parking lot.

"Are you hungry?" Steve asked as we got back into the car.

"Starving," I admitted, though until that moment I hadn't thought about food. We'd brought along a picnic lunch of cold fowl, crusty bread, cheese, oranges, and a dessert of the "Oriental sweets" I so liked. Something like baklava, they were flaky pastry rich with nuts and honey.

Palms fringed the stone remains of Memphis as, sitting on pieces of a temple column, we devoured our banquet. As we ate, we talked.

"What's been happening in Tualatin?" Steve asked, referring to the suburb of Portland where I lived. He'd been there to visit me twice since my move to Oregon from Bellevue.

"It's growing fast, and I'm not sure your country suburb image still fits, even though fields continue to abut the town. I have the horrible feeling that housing and other developments will gobble up all that wonderful farmland around Tualatin, and it makes me sad."

"I suppose the houses are the big kind that don't fit their lots proportionately."

"Some of them are, but they aren't as pretentious as in some of the other suburbs, where three- and even four-car garages seem to be de rigeur in some subdivisions. Tualatin has some great family neighborhoods."

"I'm almost afraid to ask. Is our filbert grove still there?"

"Oh yes, and I pray some developer won't chop

it down. Sometimes when I'm driving along Sagert Road, I worry that I'll spot a 'For Sale' sign on that acreage, but so far that hasn't happened, thank heavens, and the grove is well-tended." I looked at Steve with a knowing smile and added, "Cows still graze in the meadow near the gas stations, by the way."

"You remembered," he said with pleasure as his hazel eyes met mine and held. With an almost childlike glee, Steve had gotten a kick out of the way the cows merged so well into suburban life.

"Do you ever miss Seattle?" he added.

"All the time. I miss the Olympics outlined against the sky in the setting sun, the locks, the water and the ferries and Smith Tower," I told him, laughing at myself. "Steve, I've got a whole list."

"Good."

He poured us bottled water and then changed the topic completely by saying, "I suppose you're curious about Diane and me."

I was. For close to a year, he and Diane had been a couple, but her name had dropped out of our conversation months ago, and I wondered what had happened. Since I wasn't sure if he had broken it off or she had—or how sorry he was about it—I hadn't fished for details. I knew Steve well and knew he would tell me when the time was right for him. Maybe that time had come.

"If you want to tell me, of course I'm curious."

"I've wanted to tell you all along."

But I'd been a grief-stricken widow and he'd hesitated? I had been so wrapped up in myself, and now I wondered if I'd missed some cues from Steve over the past months that might have signaled his desire to talk about Diane.

Putting my glass aside, I said, "Steve, I'm sorry I've

been so self-centered. I've never stopped caring."

"I know you haven't. Lissa, that's not what I meant. You've been doing some heavy thinking, some major readjusting. You aren't self-centered for that. On a much smaller scale, I've also been thinking and adjusting, and it really hasn't been the right time for me to talk about Diane."

"I understand."

"The long and short of it is that she just isn't the woman I thought she was. Call me old-fashioned, if you will, but I'm the wife and kids and cocker spaniel by the hearth type of guy, and she seemed that way, too, at first. She liked to make gourmet meals and do needlepoint, which seemed very domestic to me, although I learned later that she didn't really like the nitty-gritty of cooking and wasn't into mending. She's also an incredibly gifted artist, Lissa, and this may sound crazy, but I think I fell in love with that facet of her personality—Diane the Artist—and just didn't let myself see the whole person. As it turned out, the person who showed so much sensitivity in her landscapes turned out not to have much in day-to-day living. It wasn't a pleasant realization, and it was a chance meeting with an old buddy of mine that woke me up. Do you remember Dave Wilkens?"

"I remember Dave," I said of a fellow who had been a quarterback when we were all in high school. "What happened?"

"Dave happened to be in the same restaurant where Diane and I were dining." Steve paused as if seeing a mental picture of the scene. "Dave was with his wife and their little boy, a Down syndrome child. The child was doing very well, Lissa, but the extra chromosome showed, and Diane was so obviously repulsed by the idea of the little boy, especially in the setting of one of her favorite restaurants, that she closed her mind to his humanness. She was quite rude to them.

"A lot started coming out after that. Diane the Artist began falling away to reveal Diane the Person. I don't know how I could have been so blind. She suddenly revealed that she didn't like people with skins of another color, she had no use for people in wheelchairs or with white canes, and she didn't even like me, really, running down my teaching because it doesn't bring in the dollars so many other professions do. To my astonishment," he said, shaking his head, "she had law school in her version of my future. In short, if Diane could have done a makeover of me, I might have made the grade."

Poor Steve! I remembered how bowled over he had been by Diane's physical beauty and her skillfully executed watercolors, and I certainly sympathized with his feeling of disillusionment.

"I'm sorry for both of you."

"Both of us? How so?"

"I feel sorry for Diane because a narrow mind is a disability of the spirit. Although her I.Q. may be fine, she's more essentially impaired in my book than Dave's little boy. Her attitude will probably catch up with her, if it hasn't already. "Besides," I went on with special feeling, "anyone who would try to remake you is not worth your time."

"That's what I decided. And me? Why do you feel sorry for me?"

"Because I know how disappointing it is not to have someone live up to your expectations."

"Here's to being ourselves," Steve said, holding out his water glass and clinking it against mine as he made his words a toast.

"To being ourselves," I echoed.

Back in our rental car, we wended our way the short

distance from Memphis to the ancient city's necropolis of Saqqara, which I knew had tombs from almost every period of Egyptian history. How sad, though, that whatever treasures had been there had been enjoyed by only a few, for the tombs had been repeatedly plundered.

As we rode along, the landscape changed so abruptly from the emerald lushness that it was startling.

"My heavens," I commented, "it's almost as if a giant had drawn a line and delegated vegetation to one side and sand to the other." No sagebrush, cacti, or visible living thing was in sight once we'd crossed the imaginary line.

"It's striking and also just a bit forbidding to see what the lack of water does."

"Oh, look at it!" I exclaimed as we suddenly got a better view of the Step Pyramid. "It looks like a gigantic sandstone wedding cake."

"A rather large one."

"How high would you say it is?" I asked. I knew it wasn't as tall as Giza's Great Pyramid, but its shape and age gave it a special aura of antiquity.

"About two hundred feet, I think," Steve told me as I thought of Imhotep fashioning it in the 3rd Dynasty. Quickly calculating and realizing that the Zoser's Pyramid was over four-and-a-half thousand years old—older even than the Great Pyramid—I shivered.

"It gives me duck bumps to see it."

"*Goose* bumps," Steve corrected automatically in what was a running mock argument between us. In my family, it had always been *duck bumps* and *goose pimples*, and the idioms had stuck.

"*Duck* bumps," I insisted playfully, incredibly happy.

To our dismay, we couldn't go inside Zoser's Pyramid that day, but we enjoyed a closer look at its six "steps" of great stone blocks, and the nearby *mastabas*, which had been private Old Kingdom tombs. Of brick and stone, with sloping walls and a flat roof, the *mastaba* had evolved into the step pyramid form and, eventually, into the true pyramid shape.

"There's a pyramid of note not far from here," Steve told me.

"Let me guess. The Pyramid of Unas?"

"Aunt Miriam's list?"

I nodded, and we exchanged smiles as we began the walk up a hill toward a pyramid two dynasties newer than Zoser's. As we reached the summit, we admired the commanding view that swept over the entire four-and-a-half mile area of Saqqara and, to the east, the greenness of palm groves and fertile fields. Once again, I noticed the invisible line that separated green from tan—literally life from death.

We entered the Pyramid of Unas by descending a sharply sloping ramp through a narrow rock-hewn passage that necessitated doubling over rather uncomfortably. Then we traversed a long, low, narrow tunnel through rock—a nightmare of a place for the claustrophobic, which fortunately we weren't—before we reached our reward of hewn chambers at the end of the passage.

Instead of finding artwork dulled by the millenia, as one might expect, we were treated to staggeringly fresh-looking stars painted on the ceiling against a background of vibrant cobalt blue, in imitation of the night sky. On the walls were the famous "Pyramid Texts," the oldest known Egyptian religious texts relating to life after death. There had been nothing like this in the Pyramid of Cheops, whose walls and ceiling were devoid of artwork, and I was thrilled by my first in-person look at ancient Egyptian art within the actual tomb.

Just before we strained to mount the steep ramp to exit, I remarked, "I'll never forget this tomb, Steve."

"Nor will I."

Our visits to the Serapeum, the Mastaba of Ti and the cat cemetery were something of an anticlimax for me.

Our final stop on the way back to Giza was a carpet school where darling raven-haired children sat three to a bench before upright looms as they tied knots in prescribed precision. Although the upper area of each loom looked like plain white threads, the lower portion had been magically transformed by the busy young fingers into the kinds of intricate designs we associate with Oriental rugs.

One little girl in particular, dressed in a bright red-print floor-length dress and wearing a hot pink scarf, caught my attention, and when our eyes met, she flashed a smile and asked for piastres by touching the palm of one hand with the forefinger of the other. Since I couldn't very well single her out, I shook my head, wishing I'd brought along a quantity of pencils, candy or other small gifts to disperse equally among them all.

"They look so young," I commented. Indeed, some looked no older than six or seven years of age.

"They are. Once they reach the age of ten, tops, their hands are too large to tie the knots with speed and precision." Steve told me that they attended school for only three hours a day and then worked for five hours. As mixed as my feelings were about that, this was a different culture. They looked well-nourished and clean, and their winning smiles seemed genuine—hardly an *Oliver Twist* setting.

"I wonder if it's hard on their eyes."

"It might be, though if you watch them, it seems that they work mainly by touch." He was right. Those little fingers seemed to fly with eyes of their own.

After watching the children work for a few more minutes, we walked into an adjacent room where the efforts of the children's labor were for sale. Rugs in all sizes and in brilliant colors such as peacock, ruby, and topaz, often of silk threads, lured the shopper. Of course the salesmen were ready to bargain, but even at rock-bottom prices, they were a little steep for a souvenir, and Steve and I decided to think about it.

Then we were on our way again.

As we approached Cairo, the sun began to stain the sky a vivid orange-rose.

"Look," Steve said, pointing to his left, where the Pyramids of Giza speared the bleeding sky, making the kind of picture one sees in *National Geographic* but rarely in person.

"How exquisite! Could we pullover and watch the sun set?"

"We certainly can. Just give me a minute to find a safe spot to pullover."

Keeping an eye on the changing sky, we rode in silence until Steve had parked the car, and finally we were outdoors watching nature's show. As we looked west, the sky subtly changed hue, one moment more beautiful than the last, making impressions one wants to bottle and keep forever. We let our cameras try to do just that.

After we had taken our fill of pictures of the travel brochure scene, we snapped a few of each other before leaning against a concrete-block wall to watch the sun sink even further. Cheops, Chephren, and Mycerinus—the trio of pyramids that had inspired so many photographs and words of praise—sat, mutely dramatic, as we watched.

"I wonder how many sunsets there have been since the pyramids were constructed," Steve mused.

"It dazzles the mind, doesn't it? What a priceless perspective it is to see the grandeur of the sky and the antiquity of the pyramids and to feel a part of it. The transience of human life is enough to make a person feel insignificant—here on earth for such a short time—and yet, yet . . . we're so very alive and aware right now," he finished for me.

The three forms had become triangular silhouettes against the colorful backdrop of sky, which was finally becoming violet.

When Steve reached for my hand, something felt different about the contact, charged as it was with new feeling, and in one fluid motion that brought us together, our lips met and held in a kiss of a kind we had never before shared.

CHAPTER SEVEN

Before the next day's sunset, on the dot of 7:30 the following evening, I was aboard the sleeper train as it departed on its overnight journey to Luxor. *Thebes!* I'd spent more than half my life dreaming about seeing Karnak and the Valley of the Kings, and now each hour drew me nearer.

But each mile also took me farther from Steve, and I had mixed feelings about that.

After our kiss as the sun set behind the pyramids, Steve and I, burningly aware of our interlaced fingers, were quiet the rest of the way back to Giza.

What was happening to me? To us? I had always cared very much for Steve, as I knew he had for me no, we'd loved each other for years, but up until now it had always been a platonic feeling. I'd never really noticed the little blond hairs on his arms or his shapely artist's hands, never wondered how it would feel to have those hands caress me. I wondered why now, of all the points in our relationship, the very thought sent a tremor through my body.

I cast a sidelong glance at him as we rode along.

Although he was twenty-seven years old, Steve had maintained a certain boyishness he'd had in high school. Had I never realized that he had turned from a boy into a man? How incredible! Suddenly, that very quality was . . . what? Appealing to me in a new way? Come on, Lissa, I told myself, say it: *sexy.*

"I'll have to let go for now," he said as we merged into heavier traffic. I thought I heard reluctance in his voice as his hand slipped gently from mine and moved toward the steering wheel.

Also reluctant to break the physical contact, I nodded, wondering what he was thinking about me as we reentered the city. Had my diminutive stature kept me every bit the high school girl to him? Was he suddenly noticing that I'd grown up and that my figure, though small-scaled, had a woman's contours?

A memory flashed to mind of a time at least a decade ago when I had gone with Steve to a shoe store to help him select a pair of slippers for his mother's birthday. We had had no trouble finding her style in the right size, but when I looked for a new pair of boots for myself in a ladies' size four, I wasn't as lucky. When the salesman had produced a similar pair in a child's size and they fit. Steve had remarked that I was going to be a little girl forever, right down to my "mouse bra."

"We're here," Steve said, cutting into the memory as we pulled into the Mena House's driveway, where two large tour buses were disgorging their riders.

Although Steve and I had originally planned to have a bite to eat in the hotel's Greenery buffet after returning, we decided we weren't very hungry after all. I didn't feel an ounce of protest in my heart when he told me he would park the car and meet me in my room, and almost in a trance, wanting and yet not wanting something to snap me awake, I followed the sidewalk across the lawn to my building.

As I entered my room and caught my reflection in the mirror, I was amazed that although an earthquake had occurred within me since morning, my tan slacks and aqua shirt were still a study in casual neatness. Except for a touch of color from the sun, I looked just as I had hours before.

I felt as nervous as a school girl as I busied myself putting away my camera and tote bag and purse. When Steve's knock came, I caught myself wondering as I thought it had come too soon and yet not soon enough, if I was doomed to have my feelings split into opposites from now on.

"Come in," I told him as I held the door open rather formally.

Too conscious of the bed taking up most of the room, I was going to suggest that we sit on the chairs near the window, or out on the balcony, when Steve spoke first.

"Let's see if Cheops is still visible," he suggested, walking toward the door leading to my second-floor balcony.

The Great Pyramid was showing all right, lit up imposingly against the night sky, and the air wafted around us playfully as, elbows touching lightly, we leaned against the railing and looked out toward the form that had sat there through the ages. What drama had it seen? What was this next installment to be?

Words drifted through my thoughts like bright confetti, but instead of catching them and turning them into the mosaic of what I felt, when I spoke it was about the pyramid.

"I like the way they're indicated the missing pyramidion," I voiced in reference to the way rods outlined the structure's original, slightly taller stature. Intensely aware of his arm scalding mine where we touched, I rattled off some facts about the tomb. Then in light of this new, still strange sexual tension between us, a laugh bubbled past my lips because it seemed very funny to be talking about a landmark when he surely must have been as aware as I was of the charged physical contact.

"What's so humorous?" he asked, looking from the pyramid to me..

"Would you believe that I'm laughing at my own prattling?"

"I love your 'prattling,' but you do that when you are nervous."

"I guess I do," I agreed, thinking how well Steve and I knew each other's little habits.

"Do I make you nervous?"

"Of course not, Steve."

"Something does."

"*Us*," I told him honestly as our eyes locked and beckoned to each other. I thought I would drown in the warm hazel depths of his.

"Let *us* make you happy, not nervous," he said as he moved away from the railing.

His open arms were a statement of their own, and I went into them gladly, letting him pull me close as I heard him huskily say, "Oh, Lissa, it feels so good—so right—to have you in my arms."

When it came, the kiss was even sweeter than the one along the road had been.

"Steve," I said softly when our lips finally parted. The name sounded brand new on my lips. "It feels good to me, too."

What an understatement! My whole body sang as I felt the length of him pressed close. Saying nothing, we stood that way for several minutes, just savoring our closeness. His lips touched my hair as my head lay against his chest, and the precious beats of his heart trotted just beneath my ear.

"Let's go back inside," he finally said, leading me gently indoors by the hand. As we passed a mirror, he stopped and wordlessly positioned me directly in front of him so that we both gazed at the reflection of a blond man a little over a foot taller than the dark-haired woman.

"Look at the way you tower over me," I said as I leaned back against him. We smiled at each others' reflections, and I wondered if he found the discrepancy in our sizes as stimulating as I did.

"You are so perfect and tiny," he murmured.

Then I was in his arms again. As we kissed, this time more urgently, his hands stroked my back, sending pulsations of pleasure through me that crescendo as one of them slipped beneath my shirt and made contact with the bare skin of my back. His heartbeats had speeded to a gallop, yet his touch was exquisitely gentle as he reached around to cup my breasts tenderly.

I was ready for him and felt his matching response. And then something happened. It seemed as if one moment I yearned for more and the next my brain cried, *Stop!*

Jeffrey. The name doused me like a cold shower, and Steve immediately felt the change in me.

"Lissa?" he questioned, obviously confused by my about-face. Arms that had a moment ago been wrapped around him dropped limply to my sides as, afraid of what I might see there, I avoided looking into Steve's eyes. I'd always despised women who turn men on and then demure at the eleventh hour. I never thought I would be one of them, never meant to be, especially not with Steve.

"Let's sit over there," I suggested as I walked toward the chairs in front of the window. I took the one closer to the wall, and Steve sat on the other. When I spoke again, if eye contact is an indication, I was talking to the refrigerator.

"I'm so sorry."

"Look at me, Lissa," he admonished when I didn't say more, but when I finally did, I burst into tears.

In two strides, he was at my side.

"Here," he said, dabbing at my eyes with a tissue before handing it to me. "I didn't mean to make you cry."

He looked so contrite as he knelt before me that I cried even harder for a moment before I reached out a hand to touch his cheek as I said, "Dear Steve, you didn't."

"Then what's wrong?" he asked as his eyes searched my face for an answer that somehow eluded even me. Perhaps he read something there. As I shook my head, he walked back to his chair.

"It's Jeffrey, isn't it?" he asked so defeatedly that I loathed myself for having put us in this position.

"In a way it is, but mostly it's me, Steve."

"What do you mean?" he asked as I wondered myself. I couldn't pin down what had disturbed me so when Jeffrey's name had dropped into my consciousness, except that Jeffrey was everywhere, still, permeating my life.

"I must be cracking up," I told Steve with a mirthless little laugh that I hoped didn't sound as insane to him as it did to me.

"Why do you say that?"

"Promise me you won't laugh?"

"Believe me, I won't laugh."

"I don't know how to put it. It's just that sometimes I have this weird feeling that Jeffrey may not be . . . well . . . not dead."

His brows arched as his forehead furrowed. Of all the things Steve had perhaps anticipated my saying, it apparently hadn't been that. He was right, though; he didn't laugh.

"Not dead? But Lissa, the authorities described the body and sent you his belongings," he reminded me not unkindly.

"You think I'm some kind of a nut, don't you?" I asked and then quietly added. "Maybe I am."

"No, I don't and you're not. I think losing your husband has been extremely traumatic."

"I never saw Jeffrey's body, Steve, never buried it, and now--" I cut myself off. Not sure I was ready to share the camel photo, I hoped Steve hadn't heard that last word. But he had.

"Now?"

The word had committed me. Without meaning to, I'd already played a terrible, if totally unplanned, sexual game with Steve, and the worst I could do now would be to play cat and mouse about Jeffrey. I reached for my purse and removed the picture. Handing it to Steve, I said, "Here, take a look at this."

For what seemed to be a very long time, he studied the snapshot before saying, "I could swear that camel is smiling, and didn't I see that look on your face the first time you parasailed?" The comment garnered a tentative smile from me since I had also fancied the dromedary to be smiling.

"Look in the background."

As I watched his eyes scan the group of men, a current of fear coursed through me, and I realized how much I banked on Steve telling me I was just reading things into the picture, that the man didn't look like Jeffrey at all. But that wasn't to be. I saw Steve's eyes lock onto the Jeffrey figure and felt my heart plummet into my intestines.

"For the love of Mike, Lissa, why didn't you show me this before?"

"You believe it's Jeffrey," I said flatly.

"I didn't say that."

"It's a pretty close likeness, isn't it?"

"Yes, it is, but you can't really believe it's Jeffrey, can you?" Maybe he saw that I did have my doubts, because his tone softened as he added, "How terrible it must have been for you to notice the man and carry this picture around."

"I'm not sure what to believe."

"Nor am I." He wore a look of resignation as he asked, "You want it to be Jeffrey, don't you?"

Did I? Of course I wanted Jeffrey to be alive. Yet if he were, what would it mean? Was he walking around with amnesia? Had he knowingly abandoned me? Was he a good person in some kind of trouble? Or was he bad through and through? Whatever the answer, one thing was certain. If Jeffrey happened to be alive, then I was still Mrs. Jeffrey Rohrer.

"I . . ." My throat felt paralyzed.

"You what?"

The words just weren't there, and all I could do was look at my feet and shake my head.

"I'd better go," he said when I didn't go on. "I'll see you for lunch tomorrow." His strange tone made me ache to erase the last hour or so, especially when I saw that this time it was Steve whose eyes wouldn't meet mine.

Almost before his words were out, he was out of his chair and halfway across the room.

"Steve," I called, startled by his abruptness. "Wait a minute." When he turned around, though, I wasn't sure what to say.

"Yes?"

"I'm sorry."

"So am I," he replied before opening the door and leaving.

The train had slowed almost to a stop, but since my watch told me it was just before midnight, I knew we were still hours from Luxor. As unrelieved blackness appeared out my window, the train rocked as it passed over a switch, and then it gradually regained its speed.

As it turned out, I never saw Steve the next day, and in light of the botched romantic interlude, I wondered if his message was an excuse not to be with me:

Dear Lissa,

Business is calling. I won't be able to meet you for lunch or in Luxor as soon as we'd planned. Have a great time. You'll love it.

I will call you at your hotel.

Love,

Steve

P.S. I thought you might enjoy this book.

The book was Florence Nightingale's *Letters from Egypt: A Journey on the Nile, 1849-1850*, a beautifully illustrated volume I'd had my eye on for some time. Touched as I was by the thoughtful gift, however, I felt deflated by the change in plans.

It also left me with some unexpected free time. I thought briefly of calling Richard Calvin, who had seemed interested in seeing me again, but although learning more about education in Egypt would be worthwhile, I realized that I did not want another encounter with my late husband's estranged college buddy at this point.

Instead, in the time I had before taking the bus to the train station, I returned to the Egyptian Museum and browsed to my heart's content. Bright with treasures, it was a rather dark, shadowy building of many rooms and deserted corners, so it was odd that when I spotted the Egyptian in the brown suit whom I'd noticed in the Church of Abu Sarga, it was as I emerged into sunshine warm enough to make the suit stand out. He quickly stepped into a cab and was gone.

Since I had some unfinished business with Asmie, I hailed a cab of my own and had it drop me off at his shop, where I told him in no uncertain terms that the charm was unsuitable.

"For the money, it is good," he told me with some truth.

People do usually tend to get what they pay for.

"That's true, but it isn't what you said you would produce," I told him in my best no-nonsense voice, thinking I might have an irate shopkeeper with whom to deal. For that reason, I was glad to see Asmie's saleswoman in the store.

Asmie surprised me, though, by merely shrugging his shoulders, retrieving Tara's cartouche, and handing back the sales slip with no further word. His lack of smile suggested that he was disgusted with me.

"Sorry for the misunderstanding," I told him as I left.

Since I had spotted a papyrus shop just down the street from Asmie's jewelry store, I stopped in and watched a demonstration of the way the ancient Egyptians had made writing material out of pressed strips of the pith of the plant. Attractive reproductions on real papyrus by contemporary scholars of ancient texts, some of which I had just seen at the museum, hung on the walls and were for sale, so I bought two to take home.

On the train, I'm not sure just when the queasiness began. Although it wasn't like me to become motion sick, in addition to the lurches at numerous switches, the train had an odd side-to-side sway that more firmly entrenched my discomfort as I rode along.

I was getting a bottle of Dramamine from my tote bag when the train rocked violently at a switch and the bag slammed against the little room's stainless steel sink. In an attempt to keep from falling, I instinctively reached out with both arms to brace myself, and as I did, I heard the bag hit the floor with a thud.

Bastet!

Hurriedly, I downed the motion sickness tablet with bottled water and then sat on the bed as I reached for my bag. At first, everything appeared to be fine. There was the feline head with its pointed ears unchipped, and the long, delicate front legs had not cracked. As I gingerly pulled the stone cat from the bag, though, its body came free from the base of the statuette—not the worst kind of breakage, to be sure, but that didn't keep me from being dismayed that Aunt Miriam's gift for Steve had been marred by my carelessness. The little form had seemed so solid.

To try to determine if it could be repaired, I set the top part down and lifted the base, gently drawing it from the bag as I had the cat's figure.

That's when I noticed the key.

Although not terribly large, it was the old-fashioned kind one might expect to find about a chatelaine's waist, to fit an *Alice in Wonderland* kind of keyhole.

What on earth?

I wondered if Aunt Miriam knew the Bastet came with a key.

Maybe it, or rather what was inside what it unlocked, was the real surprise for her nephew.

The Dramamine was making me drowsy. Just before I dozed off, I replaced the two pieces of the Bastet into my bag and put the key into the make-up pouch inside my purse.

By dawn, after a fitful half-dozen catnaps, I was still thinking in terms of airsick bags when the train reached civilization.

CHAPTER EIGHT

lthough I had never expected to pull into Luxor feeling too sick to fully appreciate my arrival, that's how it went. The sugar cane and other warmer latitude crops in the farmland near the town, houses with colorful drawings on their sides chronicling and proudly proclaiming their owners' journeys to Mecca, and Luxor Temple itself as I passed through the town on the way to my hotel—all were vague images as I fought down waves of nausea.

I smiled wanly when a stiffly formal little boy in a scarlet uniform greeted me as I entered my hotel. Then I checked in as quickly as I could and wasted no time in getting into bed once I'd reached my room.

Eating scantily from room service orders of bland foods, I fought for two days to get over what seemed to be an exaggerated case of motion sickness rather than the flu or "pharaoh's revenge." It was as if each time I tried to walk, my brain so well remembered the steady side-to-side motion and the occasional lurching of the train that it fooled itself into thinking I was still aboard. Never had I experienced anything remotely like it. Forced to stay in bed, sleeping only fitfully, I had strange dreams that included camels, Jeffrey, a Bastet with a key inside, and Steve.

As I stared at the room's papyrus-print wallpaper, I wondered again if business had really called Steve away. Or had he canceled because he was disgusted with what had happened in my room after our return from Memphis?

Why couldn't I be free?

"You're haunting me, aren't you, Jeffrey" I whispered in the empty room.

When I felt a bit better the following morning, I tried calling Steve but got no answer.

I also noticed the view for the first time. Although my room's window was set at an odd angle and afforded a better look at the pool than anything else, I could see just enough of the jutting mass of cliff across the Nile to unmistakably identify it as the area into which nestled the fabled tombs in the Valley of the Kings.

My balance, although steadier, still wasn't quite back to normal, however, so I stayed in again. As I finally had a sound sleep that afternoon, my dreams began to include scenes along the lines of Egyptian royalty in solar barques on their way to worship the great sun deity, Amun-re, at Karnak, whose massive pylons were decked out with festival flags.

I slept like a log that night.

The following day, I felt almost back to normal, if a bit weak, and decided to celebrate feeling more human again with lunch in one of the hotel's restaurants. I had just finished my fruit and cheese plate and was sipping iced tea when I heard a small voice.

"I remember you from the train," it came, startling me since I didn't immediately see its owner.

As I looked over my left shoulder, a little girl eight

or nine years old with spun-gold hair walked around so that I could see her. I wanted to be able to tell her that I remembered her from the train, too, but I couldn't.

"Hello," I greeted. "Would you like to sit down and have a cola while I finish my tea?"

While she hesitated, I thought what a beautiful child she was. Her features were exquisitely delicate, matching her small-framed body, and the cascade of hair ran like a molten river over tanned shoulders bared by her sleeveless blouse. She seemed to be studying me too.

"All right," she said as her large purplish-blue eyes met mine.

She pulled out the chair opposite mine and sat down. We ordered her drink.

"My name is Lissa. What's yours?"

"Lauren."

"That's a lovely name."

After the waiter set the soft drink in front of the little girl, she took a sip before asking, "Do you know why I remember you from the train?"

How sober she was, I thought, as I caught a certain preoccupation in the way she sat and looked.

"Let's see," I said. "Is it because I'm a shrimp?"

"No," she succinctly replied, not helping me out much. "Then it must be because I'm so funny looking," I told her.

"No, no," she protested, finally breaking into a smile. "I remember you because you were carrying Florence Nightingale's book, and I want to be a nurse when I grow up. Are you a nurse?"

"No, I'm not, but I can't think of a better profession, Lauren, except maybe for teaching. Perhaps that's because I'm a teacher and love my work. If I hadn't become a teacher, though, I think I might have been a nurse myself. Is there a special reason why nursing appeals to you?"

She took a deep swig of pop, wiped her mouth with her hand, and said, "I like to help people." She paused in a way that told me she might be debating about how much to tell me. Apparently deciding that I was safe, she added, "I was a premature baby, and I want to be a pediatric nurse and help other babies like they helped me. Only now it might not work out."

Despite her soberness, her eyes had been clear and bright. Now I thought I saw sadness suddenly veil them. As much as I wanted to ask her why she thought it might not work out, I didn't feel that I knew her well enough to probe. She would tell me if she wanted to.

"You have many years to decide," I told her. "Helping people is certainly a wonderful reason to be a nurse. The right reason, I'd say."

From across the room, I saw a couple who were probably in their late sixties approaching our table just then, though since her back was to them, Lauren couldn't see them coming. The child jumped when, closer to us, the woman called, "There you are, Lauren, It's time to leave for the museum."

The woman (Lauren's grandmother, perhaps) had a kind look. Fairly tall, she was large-boned without being heavy, and her brown eyes and salt-and-pepper hair, cropped short, were no-nonsense yet not severe.

"I hope you didn't mind the company," she said to me.

"Not at all," I assured her. Then to the child I said, "We had a nice talk, didn't we, Lauren?"

She nodded.

"We're the Brenners," the very sunburned male half of the couple said, "Lauren's grandparents."

"From St. Louis," added Mrs. Brenner.

Addressing them both, I said, "I'm Alyssa McKinnon . . . Lissa for short—from Oregon."

"That's a beautiful place," Mr. Brenner commented. He was so badly burned that even the simple mechanics of talking looked painful as the reddened skin stretched over his cheeks. Although his hair had faded, I was willing to bet that at one time he'd been a blazing redhead.

"Won't you sit down?" I asked.

"Not this time, but thanks," he told me. "We were just leaving for Luxor Temple and the museum."

"The shuttle's probably here right now, in fact, Lissa," his wife added, "so forgive us if we rush off."

"That's perfectly all right," I assured her. "Have a nice time."

"Thanks," they chorused.

Lauren had been quiet as her grandparents and I exchanged greetings, and not wanting her to feel left out, I looked into her eyes so that she'd know I was addressing her in particular and said, "I'll look for you tomorrow."

"You will?" she asked, looking pleased but skeptical.

I nodded my head emphatically as I replied, "You can count on it."

After waving them off, I finished my tea and then went back to my room for my hat and sunglasses. Suddenly, I felt well enough to see some of Aunt Miriam's Luxor area must-sees, and I knew exactly where I wanted to start: Karnak, the dazzling architectural creation of a storied past where rulers spanning centuries had added something—a pylon here, an obelisk there—to honor the Theban triad of Amun, Mut and their son Khons.

With mounting excitement, I could see the massive stone towers of the First Pylon growing larger as I approached Karnak down a tree-lined avenue. The bus from the hotel deposited me near a small booth where I purchased my entrance ticket, and then I was on my way.

I walked across a footbridge and, as I stood in the impressive Avenue of Rams just in front of the towers that dominated the entrance, felt whispering around me a distant past that encompassed anywhere from around 2,000 B.C. to shortly before Christ was born, when most of the building activity had taken place. Images of ancients hauling stones, artisans carving reliefs, and grand pharaonic processions floated through my thoughts like elaborate ghosts.

The stone rams to either side of me wore an air of benign defiance of the eras gone by, and even with real black goats munching on tufts of grass at the bases of two of them, the statues lost none of their regal bearing.

My eyes traveled to the opening between the two towers. Even though I had known that Karnak was an enormous temple complex covering some two hundred acres, I was awed as I looked down the vast length that went to and through the Great Court, the Great Hypostyle Hall, and on to the Great Temple of Amun.

"The First Pylon is Ethiopian," I remembered Aunt Miriam saying as I walked between its towers, "and just notice those walls when you go through. They are some forty-nine feet thick." As I passed through, I also noticed ancient mud brick ramps for hauling stones still visible behind the unfinished south tower.

The Great Court seemed even larger than I had imagined. There were colonnades on both sides, more figures of rams, and various temples and chapels in or adjacent to the huge open expanse, which I would explore on a subsequent visit. For now, mindful that this was only my first afternoon out of bed, I settled for a self-styled mini-tour of the sprawling complex, vowing to return soon to examine Karnak's nooks, crannies and overwhelmingly rich details.

What I came away with as I walked among forests of columns, magnificent reliefs and statues, and entire temples was an enormously satisfying sense of wonderment at Karnak's grand scale and sense of overlapping history. The gargantuan Temple of Amun, for instance, represented the building activities of many successive rulers of Egypt, with considerable one-upmanship as they vied with one another for impressive additions.

In the great open spaces where the afternoon sun streamed down, as well as in shady spots where the sun kissed only particular features, centuries fell away so that Amun-re was still a god.

It was in one of these bright open places that a shadow crossed my day as I was contemplating the majesty of an obelisk piercing the exceptionally blue sky. As I considered what it must have been like when, as worthy first resting places of the daily sun, obelisks had been gilded with electrum, an alloy of gold and silver, a human figure slipped by and caught my eye.

It was the old-fashioned baggy-trousered brown suit amidst all the casual tourist attire that did it. Although I felt no sense of danger, I did feel a twinge of uneasiness to have run into the same man at the Church of Abu Sarga, the Egyptian Museum and now Luxor, which was hundreds of miles from Cairo.

At least this time I got a good look at his face before he melted into another area of the temple complex. Maybe my eyes were playing tricks on me, but the middle-aged, balding

Egyptian seemed to have the kind of high cheekbones and other facial features I had seen in artwork portraying some of the ancient Egyptians.

Whatever the case, I was getting tired, so I consulted the map in my guidebook and made my way to the Sacred Lake, where I knew there was a rest stand. A cold drink would hit the spot, I thought as I reminded myself to bring along bottled water next time.

Maybe it was because I was tired, but the slightly saline lake was disappointing, looking rather stagnant and ordinary in the late afternoon light. The small bazaar at the water's edge, although it carried some excellent postcards, also did little to further the lake's sacred image.

I'd done too much and decided to call it a day.

I was about halfway through my dinner when I saw Lauren and Mrs. Brenner enter the crowded hotel dining room. As Lauren looked down at her shoes, her grandmother scanned the room in search of a vacant table. I looked, too, and didn't see any, so as the twosome looked my way, I waved them over. They seemed pleased by my offer to share a table.

"Cramps looks like a lobster," the child informed me as she took the chair opposite mine. She had changed from shorts into a lavender gingham sundress that accentuated her blonde fragility.

"I'm sorry to hear that," I told her as I also made eye contact with her grandmother, who had taken the chair next to Lauren's. "He did look pink earlier."

Mrs. Brenner said, "That rascal never listens. He does this every time we travel."

As the three of us shook our heads at Mr. Brenner's lack of caution, we talked a bit about the intensity of the sun in Upper Egypt, agreeing that the summer months must be very uncomfortable.

"Lauren tells me that you're a school teacher, Lissa," Mrs. Brenner said. "What grade do you teach?"

"Fifth."

"I'll be in fifth grade this fall," Lauren said.

"It's a good grade to be in. I wish you were going to be in my class."

"So do I," she told me a bit wistfully. "I'll probably get Mrs. Hartzell."

What a fate! I thought.

"She's a very good teacher," the grandmother put in. "Your dad had her, too."

Lauren rolled her eyes.

While they walked over to the buffet table, I ordered another pot of tea. Enjoying their company, I was in no hurry to leave.

As they ate, we filled each other in on what we'd seen that afternoon, and then talked about our respective parts of the United States. I had never been to St. Louis, though I was familiar with the Lake of the Ozarks in that state from when my grandparents from Chicago were still alive. I'd gone with them several times to the lake, to a resort called Old Hickory. Although Mrs. Brenner and her granddaughter had not been to Old Hickory, it turned out that they, too, had fished the lake, which gave us a springboard to talk about fishing for bass.

"Do you bait your own hook?" Lauren asked.

"I do," she added proudly.

"Good for you. I usually do, too, but to tell you the truth," I winked, "I don't like that part as well as reeling in a big one."

"I'm with you one hundred percent there, Lissa," Mrs. Brenner told me. "I really enjoy getting out on the lake, especially with a good plug."

We then discussed the merits of Hula Poppers and other plugs. "Minnows are best," Lauren insisted, and we smiled at the little girl, who looked far less sober than she had earlier in the day.

"Have you been to Egypt before, Lissa?" Mrs. Brenner asked as she sipped coffee. She was eating lightly because she found the food overly spiced, but Lauren, I noticed, was putting it away like a stevedore.

"No, this is a first for me," I told her. "Except for Greece, I haven't been abroad before."

"Oh Greece!" the woman said longingly. "I hope to get there one day."

"It's a lovely country," I said, thinking about the range of beautiful scenery and wealth of ancient splendors. "'The realms of gold,'" I mused.

"Realms of gold," Lauren repeated slowly, seeming to savor the phrase.

"It's from a famous poem," I explained.

"Say it to me," she requested, and I repeated the melodic lines of Keats's "On First Looking into Chapman's Homer."

"That's beautiful," Mrs. Brenner commented as I saw that Lauren also liked it. "Lauren," she told the child, "I have a volume of Keats's poetry at home. Would you like to look through it once we get back?"

Lauren nodded, but if her creased forehead and downcast eyes were any indication, something troubling had suddenly crossed her mind, and her grandmother and I exchanged puzzled glances.

Conversation stalled after that. Thinking that it was

time for me to return to my room, I was on the verge of
getting up when Mrs. Brenner spoke. "What are you doing
tomorrow?" she asked.

"It's going to be the Valley of the Kings for me," I told
her enthusiastically.

The little girl came back to life with, "Oh, the Valley
of the Kings! I wish I could go there tomorrow, but Gramps
has to stay indoors for a while."

I could tell that Lauren ached to get to the Valley. I did
some quick thinking and asked her grandmother, "Is your
husband well enough to be left alone?"

"Yes, he's miserable but basically all right."

"Why don't you and Lauren come along to the Valley
with me tomorrow? I'd be happy to have you as company,
and you could return with him after he's feeling better," I
said.

"Can we, Grandma?" Lauren asked, and I could sense
her mentally crossing her fingers.

"Well . . . are you sure, Lissa?"

"Very," I told them, looking from one to the other.

CHAPTER NINE

Armed with sunblock, bottled water and hats to protect us from the uncompromising rays of the sun as the day wore on, Lauren and I, equally excited, left the hotel for the boat dock by bus in the morning coolness. Mrs. Brenner, after making sure I wouldn't mind taking just her granddaughter, had decided not to go with us, and I imagined that her husband would appreciate her company.

"It's miserable to be sunburned," I commented to Lauren in the bus. As fair-haired as the child beside me was, her skin tanned well, so maybe she had been spared from ever having known that particular agony. I, on the other hand, had dark hair and fair skin I had to baby.

"I guess so. Poor Gramps," she said with feeling. Then, "Do you want to know a secret?"

"If you want to tell me, I'm all ears," I told her, cupping one ear with my hand.

"Grandma's really afraid to be in tombs. She doesn't like closed-in places and freaks out."

"That puts her in plenty of company," I told her. I was terrified of rats myself and would be the last person to judge a claustrophobic. Since we would be in plenty of tombs that day, though, I needed to find out if the child shared her grandmother's discomfort, so I asked, "How about you, Lauren? Will the tombs bother you?"

"Oh no! I can hardly wait! I love spooky things," she said forcefully.

As we crossed the Nile by steamer, the little girl and I quietly pondered the imposing mass of rock cliffs as we drew near the west bank. I also thought how in all my daydreams of visiting the fabled Necropolis of Thebes, never had I pictured myself with a nine-year-old girl as company. I hoped it wouldn't be a mistake. Somehow, I sensed that our day together was going to be fine, for there had been that longing in Lauren's voice last evening when she'd uttered "the Valley of the Kings"—a longing that reminded me of myself at that age.

I would be returning to the Valley later, at any rate, for a second, probably more thorough look.

"Look at all the buses," Lauren remarked as we looked from the dock to an area where possibly the largest congregation of the vehicles I had ever seen at a tourist attraction waited for the steamers to unload tomb visitors.

"There must be twenty-five or thirty," I commented.

As we made our way to that area, a wizened man in a white galabia approached, hawking souvenirs, and on impulse I bought two two-inch high black cat figures that were miniatures of the much heavier Bastet I was toting in my bag. I wasn't sure of the latter's worth and did not feel comfortable leaving it in my room. Although I might have left it at the front desk, Lauren had not had breakfast when we met, and by the time she'd eaten, our bus was waiting and I had missed my chance.

"Here," I told the little girl, handing her one of the tiny

cat figures as I slipped the other into my jeans pocket, "now we'll each have something from the Valley of the Kings."

Lauren's gigantic blue eyes lit up in obvious pleasure as, thanking me, she examined the sleek little cat.

We looked for the bus that matched our coupons and were soon on our way to the necropolis.

The lifelessness of the landscape held us in awe. It looked so totally inhospitable.

"It looks like a pebbly desert with cliffs," Lauren remarked as we rode along. As she drank in the view, she stroked the little Bastet.

"I know. It's so empty and dry. Isn't it hard to imagine the ancient workers coming here and carving out chambers and then decorating them in this lonely place?"

She nodded and added, "And bringing the mummies and all their tomb stuff."

As I wondered how many of the laborers had succumbed to heatstroke, I knew we were fortunate not to be here in high summer when the searing heat made climbing in the steep, rocky terrain, unshaded except for within the tombs themselves, very fatiguing. Even in the relative coolness of early spring, the day would turn hot.

We began our tour in an area of the necropolis called the Valley of the Queens, where, among others, we visited the Tomb of Queen Titi and walked through the many chambers of Queen Nefertari's. When a guide briefly doused the lights and cast us into pitch darkness in one of the tombs, Lauren and I enjoyed the deliciousness of a supremely "spooky" moment. To me, "as dark as a tomb" became more than just a phrase, and I was rather glad to have her warm little hand holding mine.

Back in the bus, we chugged our way to the magnificent temple complex of Deir el-Bahri, built in the

New Kingdom reign of Queen Hatshepsut. Three terraces linked by stone ramps gave the whitish sandstone temple a dramatic appearance against its backdrop of steeply scarped honey-colored cliffs. We stopped to take several pictures before climbing the first ramp.

Once inside, Lauren was indignant that Hatshepsut's visage and name had been obliterated repeatedly throughout the temple.

"How could they erase her name like she never was? Was it tourists?" she asked, apparently as unimpressed as I was with the rude behavior of some of them. This time, though, they were hardly the culprits.

"No, Lauren. It was politics," I explained as I gave her a nutshell account of how Hatshepsut, the daughter of Tuthmosis I, had become the wife of her stepbrother, Tuthmosis II. She had acted as regent on behalf of Tuthmosis III, her stepson, before becoming Queen in her own right. After her death, however, her stepson became sole ruler and erased her name and likeness, such as through chiseling them off reliefs, wherever he could.

"That makes me sad," Lauren said with a preoccupied look that seemed to go deeper than the issue at hand, especially when she added, "People do that today. They throw things away and put away all the pictures. Poor Queen Hatshepsut."

With Lauren screwing up her face in distaste each time we ran across a marred image of the woman, I couldn't help remembering the Allerton Collar and wondering if its existence were fact or fiction.

Aunt Miriam had told me the story of Thomas Allerton, who in the 1940s had, by his own account, made a stunning find—a fabulous necklace of gold and alternating rows of lapis-lazuli and carnelian that had belonged to

Hatshepsut. Beautiful beyond belief as Allerton described it, it had disappeared, as he himself had, and no one had seen the collar since.

Had it even been real? With so much evidence of disrespect for the Queen around me, I doubted that any pains would have been taken to preserve her jewelry intact, but one never knows. Someone who loved or admired her might have.

Fortunately, despite the defacement of Hatshepsut's name and likeness, other artwork in the temple complex had been left alone, and Lauren and I enjoyed looking at beautiful reliefs in, for instance, the Chapel of Anubis, the jackal-headed god, with whom my young companion seemed familiar. She also recognized the Hathor-headed columns in another part of the complex.

"Cow-headed," she said, amused by the womanly head with cow's ears.

As we left the temple and descended the last ramp, Lauren remarked, "Those dogs are chasing that man."

She was right. Even though the day was heating up, dogs that had earlier seemed to be listlessly lounging near the entrance had come to life.

"They must be temple dogs, Lauren, and I think their job is to round up stray people, perhaps so they won't get lost or enter certain areas." Sturdy, medium-sized and usually about the same color as the cliff face that rose behind us, the dogs had counterparts at many other temple sites.

We drank bottled water in the bus on the way to the Valley of the Kings, where many of the sixty-four discovered tombs turned out not to be open to the public at all or temporarily closed for restoration. What we saw left us in thrall, however, offering a visual picnic of passageways adorned with priceless artwork, burial chambers where mummies had rested in splendor "for all time," and series of interconnected rooms whose size and number within a tomb indicated that particular pharaoh's stature in life.

After we had visited several of them and were outside again, I said, "Let me take your picture in front of this sign, Lauren."

Without reading it, she obediently posed for me. Her head didn't reach the pointed directional marker that read TOMB OF TUTENCHAMUN NO 62.

"Tuten--," she started to say after I snapped two pictures.

She had turned around to read the marker and was at first puzzled by the different spelling of the familiar name. Her expression brightened when she figured it out. "Oh, King *Tut!*"

"That's right," I told her, knowing this was the tomb that intrigued Lauren the most. "Shall we go there next?"

"Oh, let's!"

Although it was push and shove near the famous tomb, we couldn't leave the Valley without seeing for ourselves what remained in the tomb itself of Howard Carter's 1922 "find of the century."

"Why are they leaving their cameras?" Lauren asked as she noticed people ahead of us handing their equipment to an attendant.

"Flashbulbs can damage some types of artwork inside tombs," I explained. In other tombs, I had seen an occasional tourist trying to cheat by taking forbidden pictures of sensitive frescos, for example, and wondered at the lack of regard for something so priceless and vulnerable. No one was leaving anything to chance inside Tomb 62, I thought, as I handed over mine.

Then suddenly we had come to the famous sixteen

steps leading down into the tomb. Although a new stairway had been constructed over the original stairs to accommodate the heavy foot traffic entering and leaving the tomb, a pleasant shiver coursed down my spine as I saw the originals below.

Lauren and I had been lumped together with a tour group whose guide was telling his people that Tutankhamun, the son-in-law of Akhenaten, had died at the tender age of eighteen or nineteen. Even though he was only a minor personage, the grave goods from his tomb had been the most valuable find of the kind ever made in Egypt. Remembering the wealth of items I had seen from the tomb, I was about to enter, I wondered what had been inside the tomb of a major pharaoh, especially that of Rameses II, and what had happened to all those goods. I knew that we had the opportunity to gaze upon the contents of Tomb 62 only because it had not been discovered, as so many had, by ancient plunderers.

Flowing ahead with the group, we walked through a doorway and then traversed a narrow passage about twenty-five feet long. Although Lauren didn't seem daunted, she stayed close to me.

"It's spooky," she whispered.

"It is," I agreed. Even though much smaller than other tombs we had visited that day, this one did have an aura—a *spookiness*, I suppose, as well as a certain familiarity, given the items we had seen in the museum that other tombs lacked.

At the end of the tunnel, we came to another doorway that led us into an antechamber. It was here that Carter had found a magnificent collection of six to seven hundred items that included clusters of alabaster vases; parts of chariots; animal-sided couches; jewelry that included an elaborate corselet of gold, carnelian and faience; beaded sandals; and the dazzling golden throne.

"We're almost there," I told the little girl. I knew from her grandmother exactly what it was that she had been wanting so earnestly to see.

"His mummy?"

I nodded.

The tomb chamber was off to the side. Both short, Lauren and I could not see into it, since a clot of tourists had crowded in front of us, and although we inched ahead, we stood blocked from a clear view for long moments that tested our patience. To be so close! As the crowd finally began to thin, we made our way over to a railing and beheld a stunning sight in the space beyond.

"Oh, there it is!" Lauren exclaimed as she got her first look beyond the railing.

"Yes, that's it," I confirmed, as awestruck as she.

The sarcophagus of yellowish crystalline sandstone lavishly covered with religious texts and scenes was before us, and although except in his likeness on the sarcophagus we could not see him, we knew the boy-king was still resting for eternity within. After my eyes had feasted upon the sight, I looked from the sarcophagus to Lauren, and her eyes were riveted to the ornate form.

"There are ladies on the corners," she said in reference to four figures of winged goddesses.

I told her what I knew about them, and then she made what seemed like a strange comment for a little girl.

"Our caskets are so plain," she said quietly, with a look of deep sadness.

As we moved away from the viewing area to allow those behind us their turn, I wondered what a nine-year-old child knew about caskets. It wasn't the time or place to ask, though, as we were being hurried along so that the next group could enter the tomb.

Although Lauren had been enjoying our excursion, she also had seemed taut with preoccupation at some points, as though nothing completely took her mind off something that deeply troubled her.

Since climbing up and down had grown tiring, especially as the day grew hotter, it seemed like a good time for a rest. Maybe I could also get Lauren to talk a little about what bothered her.

"Would you like to sit and just talk for a while?" I asked as we emerged from the tomb. "The calves of my legs are beginning to scream," I added as I reclaimed my camera.

"Scream?" A trace of amusement animated her face.

"Hurt," I explained, "no doubt from so much climbing."

"Okay," she said.

We made our way to the nearby rest-house, where I bought cold drinks and carried them to a tiny table. Sitting down felt heavenly.

"So, Lauren, how do you like the Valley of the Kings?"

"I love it, Lissa," she said unhesitatingly. She looked more relaxed than she had been a few minutes ago. "I like the spooky tunnels and all the pretty drawings on the walls and the sar . . ."

"Sarcophagus," I supplied.

"I like the sarcophagus where King Tut's mummy is." She seemed to be seeing it again in her mind's eye. Then the light of enthusiasm flickered low as she frowned and began what seemed to be another train of thought. Only. . . ."

"Only?" I questioned gently as I smiled at her reassuringly when she didn't continue.

"What happens if people don't remember a dead person's name and the person wasn't made into a mummy for all time, with all his stuff to help him in the other world?"

The thought of Jeffrey's body, "taken care of" somewhere and somehow in Turkey, arrowed into my consciousness uncomfortably.

I pushed it away as best as I could. What could I say to this little girl who had asked such a forthright and, I could tell, burning question, when I still searched for answers of my own?

"To tell you the truth, Lauren," I began tentatively, "I don't really know. The religion of ancient Egypt is a very, very old one. Many new ones have begun since that time, including Christianity and Islam. I can't imagine that one religion is more right than another, and I think a dead person's spirit goes somewhere good—a place we can't really know—when he or she dies, regardless of what's done with the body."

But hadn't I been hung up to some extent upon bodies myself? Not having buried Jeffrey's had left something unfinished for me. "He was only a boy, wasn't he?" Lauren asked.

"Do you mean King Tut?"

"Mmm-hmm."

"Yes, though older than you by several years."

"But he was Pharaoh."

"That's right, and it must have been a huge responsibility for a young man."

"You're sad about something, aren't you, Lissa?" she asked. I had been so intent upon observing Lauren that her astute observation surprised me.

Sad. There was that word again, a word which didn't really describe the potpourri of emotions surrounding Jeffrey's sudden death, my discoveries afterwards and, now, the direction of my relationship with Steve. *Sad?* Yes, I was sad sometimes. But I was also hurt, angry, enormously disappointed, and confused—not necessarily in that order or all at once.

"Yes, sometimes I am sad," I admitted. "Someone I loved, my husband, died last year."

"Was it your fault?" she asked, startling me.

My fault! Why ever would she think my husband's death was my fault? And was it? No, no, and a thousand times no! I had already answered that question after hour upon hour of painful soul-searching. I'd done the right thing by staying home on that fatal trip of Jeffrey's. I had had a responsibility to my marriage, to be sure, but so had he, and we had agreed before marrying that I would continue teaching for at least a few more years. Even to accommodate the man I loved, I couldn't in all conscience have breezed off to Turkey during the school year without advance arrangements.

"No, Lauren," I told the little girl. "He died in an accident far from home."

"Oh," she said, "I'm sorry," and something in her tone, in her un-childlike look of empathy, made me realize that perhaps someone she loved had also died.

Very gently, I asked, "Did someone you love die, too, Lauren?"

When her small gasp of surprise told me I was on the right track, I added, "It's very hard, isn't it?"

She blinked her large delphinium-blue eyes and nodded. "Would you like to tell me about it?"

"I don't know," she said. As I had in the restaurant yesterday, I could almost see the debate going on within her as her pale brows knit and she wrinkled her forehead. This time the internal struggle seemed keener, and I was relieved when she finally said, "Yes, I want to tell you about Jason."

When she stopped, however, as if she didn't know how to go on, I prompted, "Jason?"

"My little brother," she explained as she looked down at her hands and studied them for a few moments before meeting my eyes again. Hers had become dark pools.

"He died. He died, Lissa," she said with sudden emotion that tensed her delicate frame, "and it's all my fault!"

With that, she was up and out of her chair, racing out of the rest-house, into the glaring afternoon sun. I grabbed my things and dashed after her.

Her thin shoulders were shaking by the time I reached her near the sign where I had taken her picture earlier, and I held her as she trembled with an anguish no child should have to endure.

What in the world? I doubted very much that she had been responsible for her brother's death, but the important thing was that Lauren felt she had been, and it was eating her up.

"I'm sorry," she sputtered as she slowly pulled away and wiped her eyes. I handed her a fresh tissue.

"You don't have to be. Tears can be good. They help us get our feelings out, and sometimes we have to do that before we can deal with them." I told her.

Since the walkways in the area were crowded, mostly with people going to Tomb 62, I suggested that we walk down by the buses, where there was also some shade. The day had grown quite hot.

"You can tell me more then if you want to," I told her as we left the tomb area.

Once there, we found some shade, and she asked, "Did you feel awful after your husband died?"

"I certainly did. I felt very alone and lost."

"But it wasn't your fault."

"No, it wasn't, and maybe Jason's death wasn't your fault, either. Maybe it just seems that way. Why do you think it's your fault?"

"I used to want a little brother or sister. Most of my friends had them, but I never did. I guess I finally stopped wanting one. Then Jason was born in November. He cried a lot, Mom was tired all the time, and Daddy only talked about having a son, like I wasn't even there any more. Sometimes I wanted it to be the way it was before Jason was born. I . . . I wished Jason would die, Lissa, and then . . . then he died."

"That doesn't make it your fault, though, Lauren," I told her, moved by her pain. Then feeling I needed more information,

I asked, "How did Jason die?"

"They called it SIDS," she told me, using the acronym for sudden infant death syndrome. "He wasn't sick or anything, and he just never woke up from his nap one day."

"That's very sad," I said. Then, "Lauren, I'll tell you something. We all have feelings now and then that just are not very noble and good. It's part of human nature. But if we don't act upon those bad feelings and make them really happen, then we haven't done anything wrong. We aren't to blame if something we thought about really happens."

She considered this with a serious look on her face, neither accepting nor rejecting my words. "They sent me away," she said so quietly that it had the impact of a shout. "I'm here with Grandma and Gramps because Mom and Daddy don't love me anymore."

How my heart ached for the poor child! I wondered how such miscommunication in a family could have happened. What were the real circumstances? Had Grandma and Gramps already planned this trip and then decided to take Lauren along to cheer her up and give her parents time to grieve? Had Lauren been neglected in the wake of her parents' loss? Or did it just seem that way to the sensitive little girl?

"Sweetheart," I told her, using the endearment I often used with my niece, "it's very hard when a mother and father lose a child. Don't you think that maybe they sent you with your grandparents because they love you and want you to have a good time? Isn't it possible that they thought it was too sad for you at home?

"I know how sad it can be at home after someone dies. I'll tell you a secret," I said, leaning closer and lowering my voice conspiratorially, "I'm here in Egypt partly because I'm working out feelings I have about my husband's death."

"You are? Why does it hurt so much, Lissa?"

"I think it's because when someone you love dies, it tears a big hole into the fabric of your life. It takes time to mend it."

"You must feel even worse," she said. "Jason was just a baby. Your husband was a grown man."

"I know, but a baby is just as important as a man. My husband had time to do and see many things. Think how sad it is when a person never gets to really experience life no first words, first steps, first day of school. With the loss of a little baby, part of the sadness is for what never will be."

Lauren seemed stricken by the words.

"Jason never even had a coloring book or made a snowball or rode a bike."

"I know," I replied as I thought about how it would be to lose a very young child. "Your parents probably think about these things and feel very sad. That doesn't mean they have forgotten you or changed their feelings for you."

"You think they still love me then?" she asked with such naked hunger in her expression that I could have shaken her parents for ever having let their daughter reach the point of doubting their love.

I took one of Lauren's delicate hands in mine and said,

"I'm sure they do, sweetheart."

Then I thought of something to which she might relate.

"My grandmother used to have a strange expression. She would say that a crumpled tissue or wadded paper was 'all whopsed up.' I don't know where that phrase came from, Lauren, but in a way when somebody dies, your whole life feels all whopsed up for a time, and it takes awhile to smooth it out again."

"All whopsed up," she echoed, and when I heard her repeat the expression, I hoped to high heaven that it wasn't some X-rated idiom my silver-haired, very proper grandmother had inadvertently acquired.

I didn't have time to ponder it further. I saw our bus driver shepherding his flock, looked at my watch and knew it was time to go back across the river.

Lauren and I were silent most of the way across the Nile.

Back on land, we caught the shuttle bus, and as it dropped us off at the Luxor Hilton, Lauren said, "I'll remember what you said, Lissa."

"Good. I enjoyed our day."

"Even if your legs are screaming?" she asked as I walked her to her room.

"Even though my legs are definitely screaming, Lauren. Thanks for going with me," I told her as we reached her room.

"Thanks for taking me. I loved every minute of it."

"See you tomorrow," we said almost in unison.

I had started back down the hall when I heard her voice again.

"Oh, Lissa," she called, "I loved Jason."

"I know."

⌣

Although at first glance, nothing looked out of place in my room, I sensed something different the moment I opened the door. It was the aroma of cherry wood tobacco, which I recognized from my grandfather's pipe smoking days during my childhood.

"Hello," I called out.

Leaving the door open, I stepped cautiously into the room. I looked everywhere a person might be hiding, including behind the drapes as I laughed nervously at myself, but I found no one.

Uneasily, I closed the door and continued to inspect my room for other telltale signs of an intruder. My clothes hung in the closet as I had left them, and my toiletries were arranged in the bathroom counter exactly as they had been that morning. When I opened the dresser drawer holding my underwear and T-shirts, however, a warning bell sounded in my mind. Although the shirts were in the precise piles of a tourist not in anyone room for too long, hadn't the orange one been on the top? Now it was in the middle of the pile.

Then I noticed the Nightingale book, which I knew I'd left on the desk. Now it was on a chair by the window. Could I have carried it there and forgotten? Since the bed had been made, I assumed a maid had been in the room, but I didn't think she would have moved my clothing within a drawer, and she certainly would not have been smoking a pipe.

Hotel thieves and an occasional maid with light fingers surely existed everywhere in the world, though nothing seemed to be missing. Perhaps someone had merely been curious and looked through my things. Since no harm had been done, I did not report my suspicion of an unwelcome guest to the front desk.

How easy it is to talk oneself out of heeding certain events.

CHAPTER TEN

Tomb dirt, I thought almost reverently as I rather reluctantly removed my soiled jeans and T-shirt. The dust of the ages was special. To soothe the *screaming* leg muscles that had amused Lauren, as well as to bathe, I decided that a long, hot soak in the tub was just what the doctor ordered. The bathtub was modern, fortunately, and there was plenty of hot water, so I allowed my mind to drift as I enjoyed the curative effect of the gently lapping water.

What a day it had been. Not only had I finally beheld tombs of ancient Egyptian royalty, but I had had an unexpectedly enlightening time with a little girl.

I wasn't sure if I believed in destiny—I've always thought, in fact, that we do the most important shaping of our futures ourselves, thereby determining our own destinies—but this time it was almost as if something (fate?) had thrown Lauren Brenner and me together so that we might help each other along with our respective journeys back into the mainstream from grief and sadness.

I considered the Brenners' situation. How heartbreaking it must be when a baby dies. Jeffrey had been cut down in his prime, which was sad, to be sure, but little Jason Brenner had never even remotely approached a prime, and that was tragic.

As much as my heart ached for Lauren, I couldn't justly criticize her parents, I realized, for even though I sensed that losing a child would be wrenching, I had no firsthand knowledge of such a loss. Never dreaming that Lauren might see it differently than they and feel rejected, Lauren's parents were perhaps in their own eyes being sensitive to their older child's needs by sending her away with her grandparents as they mourned their baby son. It must be a very heavy load to love, to lose, to grieve personally and also watch a surviving child grieve.

I so hoped that Lauren would transcend her feeling of guilt and move ahead bravely, wholly, to the rest of her life.

And what about you, kiddo? I asked myself. Are you moving ahead or only running on a treadmill? With a start, I realized that something in today's conversation with the nine-year-old Lauren had released me, beginning to free me from the muck of emotions that had been holding me fast for so long.

Just as Lauren had felt responsible for her baby brother's sudden death, I had fallen into a similar trap, blaming myself and sabotaging any progress I might have made with nebulous *if onlys.*

If only I'd quit teaching . . .

If only I'd gone on that last trip with Jeffrey . . .

If only I'd known what was really in his mind . . .

And *if only* I'd molded myself into just the person Jeffrey had wanted me to be . . .

All the *if onlys* merely held me fast in the mire.

Had I gone with Jeffrey to Turkey, it's possible he would still be alive today, but that didn't make me wrong for staying home and honoring my commitment to my school and my students, nor did it make me responsible for my husband's death any more than Lauren was for Jason's.

I was beginning to see that Jeffrey and I had had some serious problems just surfacing in our marriage that probably would have gotten worse had he lived. I could better myself, to be sure, but I could no more remake myself than Steve could by scrapping his profession for Diane and going to law school to meet her standards. I admired Steve for not knuckling under. I needed to give myself a break, too.

Just as Steve had his own personality and standards, which included empathy for a Down syndrome family, so did I, and for the most part, they had been set long before Jeffrey appeared on the scene. I'd determined many years ago that teaching was a vital component for me at this stage of my life, and Jeffrey had come into our marriage seemingly proud of his teacher-wife. We'd agreed that my career fit into the life we were building together as well as his did.

What if I had called his writing piddling, as he had my teaching? Had he really expected me to drop everything to travel at his side on business trips? Couldn't he just as well have changed his own work by getting a job that didn't entail frequent absences? The difference was that I never expected him to, never would have dreamed of asking him to change a line of work he loved simply to feed my own needs.

As I let some additional hot water trickle into the tub, a collage of memories flashed before me that might have been entitled *Jeffrey Gets His Way*. Except for my adamant stance on the teaching issue, I realized with a sick feeling that I'd been so quick to please my husband that I had given

him his way repeatedly, which was okay to some extent, I
suppose, but how often in our brief marriage had he asked
me what I wanted to do or how I felt? One piece of the
collage was Vesuvius, an Italian restaurant that served the
best manicotti I've ever eaten and which I had patronized
semi-regularly for years. Jeffrey's "I don't like Vesuvius,"
based upon its rather hokey atmosphere, had been it, even
when I'd played up my old haunt's strengths. Since he knew
I liked it, what would have been wrong with our going there
occasionally? For my sake, couldn't he have forced himself
and been gracious about it? Apparently not, as Vesuvius had
remained blacklisted.

Another piece of the collage concerned my young
niece, Tracy, whose parents had decided to keep the amount
of sugar their daughter ate to a bare minimum, which was
certainly their privilege. Jeffrey, however, had repeatedly
ignored their principles by arming himself with an arsenal
of sweets when we got together, and of course the little girl
had succumbed to temptation. I remembered Tracy's mother
having sat Jeffrey down after the very first candy orgy to
explain their views. Jeffrey's response had been, "Let me
have my fun." It had become such a contest that our visits
with my brother and his family had tapered off. I couldn't
get Jeffrey to budge.

Even my clothes hadn't suited him. My wardrobe
included a few of the turkeys we all seem to get stuck with—
and Jeffrey did have impeccable taste since he himself
always looked ready for a magazine photo layout—but
generally speaking, I knew what suited my small frame and
which colors flattered me. His *Are you going to wear **that**?*
had spoiled many an outfit I liked, and my wardrobe had
changed in the months of our marriage, especially as to
color. Jeffrey did not like blue, which had always been my

best color, so, increasingly, my blue clothing had stayed in my closet.

I saw now that the vasectomy fit into this collage. Just as he had seemed proud of my career, so had he seemed as full of dreams as I about the small family we one day hoped to have. Then he destroyed them by sneaking off to end his fertility.

Had Jeffrey changed that much or had he been someone I only thought I knew? Had he lived, what else would have gone into the collage to contradict the man I thought I'd married?

As I reclined in the tub, I realized that because I had made unpleasant discoveries about Jeffrey posthumously, when he was no longer there to supply the answers I craved, I had to leave many of them unanswered, perhaps for all time. I'd drive myself around the bend for sure if I were to try to second-guess my late husband. It was time to accept my deep disappointment in him, remember the good times, and let go.

"Jeffrey is dead," I said aloud as the sound of my voice echoed around the room.

As I finally lathered myself with soap, although I ached over each discovery of a Jeffrey I hadn't really known, I felt more hopeful than I had for eleven months. I *was* moving ahead.

I felt so much better after my long soak that I put on a rose-colored jersey dress and decided to treat myself to dinner at the Winter Palace, which is how I happened to see Richard Calvin.

I had finished my *kofta*, a meatball dish whose spicy sauce I found delicious, and had just made a restroom stop off the grand old hotel's lobby on my way out when as I emerged, Jeffrey's old college chum just happened to be walking through.

Our eyes met for only the merest fraction of a second, it's true, but I thought I caught the flicker of recognition. I was about to walk toward him in greeting when he quickened his pace, walked outside and hastily disappeared into a cab after descending the hotel's wide front steps.

Perhaps it wasn't that unusual. Since Luxor must make a romantic getaway for the lucky Cairoans who could afford to travel, maybe Richard had a secret affair going.

Back in my room, I was relating my trip to the Valley of the Kings in a letter to my parents when the shrill of the telephone broke into my thoughts.

"Hello," I answered.

"Lissa, it's Steve," came the voice that in the wake of his hurried departure from my hotel room in Giza, I had both longed and dreaded to hear. To my relief, he sounded as he always had.

"Hi, Steve."

"How is everything in Thebes, and what did you see today?"

"I'm having a wonderful time," I told him, omitting mention of my motion sickness. "Today it was the necropolis with a little American girl whose grandfather looks as though he'd been parboiled. He needed some time indoors. Lauren is sweet, and I think I saw the tombs with a nine-year-old's sense of wonder as well as from my own not any less enthusiastic perspective."

"I'll bet she found the tombs spooky," he said. Although Steve taught at the college level, he'd always liked children and had a good sense of what they liked and felt at various ages.

"She did, and you should have seen the way her eyes lit up when she saw Tutankhamun's sarcophagus."

We talked then about particular tombs before Steve asked, "What do you think of Karnak?"

"Ah Karnak! What can I say?"

"Maybe your sigh says it best. It's a marvelous spot, isn't it?"

"It certainly is. What a sense of history it imbues."

"I know. I was awestruck my first time there. The great thing is that with Karnak, it gets even better on successive visits. After the initial impact of the scope of the temple complex starts to wear off, details you hadn't noticed before begin to emerge."

Had we given ourselves free rein, we might have talked about tombs and Karnak for an hour, but this was long distance, and I wanted to shift the conversation, anyway, to a topic that I knew mattered to us both in a very different way from temples and tombs.

"Steve," I began, stopping almost involuntarily after his name as I was struck again by how different it felt on my lips than it had before the sunset kisses. I hadn't meant to insert an audible pause, but apparently he detected it. "Lissa?" he queried.

"I'm still here," I assured him with a warning to myself to get on with it this time. "I'm sorry about my flight of fancy the other night. Of course Jeffrey is dead. You know I've had trouble all along believing it, and I suppose that's why I read things into that camel picture."

"Yes, as early as the night I broke the news to you, I remember your insistence that there had been a mistake."

"I think I'm getting over that. The little girl I mentioned also lost someone recently, and believe it or not, she has helped me accept the fact that people do die prematurely, sometimes a lot more so than Jeffrey."

"I'm glad to know you are feeling better about it, Lissa. I know it's been rough."

When he didn't continue, I decided that maybe that was all there was to say about it for now. It wasn't the time to ask him how he felt about us, but I longed to pepper him with questions about his feelings. More than anything else, I wanted his assurance that we hadn't irretrievably damaged our essential relationship with a complication that might tear down vital elements of what we had built over the years.

I searched for a neutral topic.

"How's your work coming along?" I asked. "Have you found some additional portals for the book?"

"As a matter of fact, I have, but . . ."

"But what?" I asked when his voice trailed off. "They're going to have to wait for a future volume."

"I hadn't realized you have almost all you need for the current book."

"Actually, I don't, Lissa."

"I don't understand."

He paused for what seemed like a long while before he finally said, "The new doors aren't in Egypt, and I saw them only in passing."

"Not in Egypt? What do you mean?" I had assumed that Steve was off to Alexandria, an oasis, or elsewhere Egyptian on the quest for new doors. "Where are they?"

"In Turkey," he said so softly that I almost didn't hear him.

But I had, and I felt the blood drain from my face. To me, Turkey was still synonymous with Jeffrey's death, a place where people suddenly cease to be. Even though my more reasonable Self told me it wasn't fair to the Turkish people, who no doubt ranged the gamut of the human spectrum,

I'd developed an unfortunate mental image of a bushy-haired Turk in a fez sorting through Jeffrey's personal effects before sending them to me, and this figment of my imagination had taken on a sinister cast in recurrent dreams.

"Turkey!" I exploded. "Why didn't you tell me you were going there?"

"I wasn't sure myself until the last minute."

"Are you still there?"

"No, I'm back in Cairo," he said, as if that explained everything.

"Stop hedging."

"I haven't meant to, Lissa."

"You're certainly not volunteering much information. Why were you in Turkey, of all places?"

Had he been anywhere but there, I'm sure I wouldn't have felt compelled to grill him. There were probably one thousand and one reasons to go to that particular corner of the world, but Steve's having gone *there* made me uneasy and raised some questions.

"Did you go for information about Jeffrey?" I asked straightforwardly, but even as I did, panic rose within me and I blurted, "You went because you were struck by the Jeffrey look-alike in that camel snapshot, didn't you?"

I heard him sigh.

"Lissa, please don't leap to conclusions."

"I'm sorry. I didn't mean to jump on you, Steve. I'm just trying to get to the truth."

"It's okay. You're understandably upset," he said with compassion in his voice that choked me up. I'd probably sounded like a fishwife. "If I seemed to be hedging," he continued, "it's because I wasn't sure I wanted to get into this on the phone and chance upsetting you again.

"I did go to Turkey for information about Jeffrey's

death, but not because I think the man in the photo is Jeffrey. I went because when I saw how upset you were the other night, I wanted to put this to rest once and for all. You deserve some peace of mind."

I was overwhelmed.

"You went all the way to Turkey to help me have peace of mind?"

"Yes, because I . . . care for you. We've been friends for what. . .?"

"Twelve years," I supplied.

"In a dozen years, you get to know somebody pretty well. I don't like what I've been seeing since Jeffrey died, Lissa. You've often seemed consumed by an emotion I can't define but which seems separate from, and somehow beyond, grief. I guess it all came to a head for me when I saw what the camel photograph had done to you."

"Maybe I'm like Lauren."

"Lauren?"

"The child I've befriended here," I explained. "It's easy to get off the track after someone dies suddenly. I know you're trying to help me get back on, Steve, and I do appreciate your trip to Turkey. It's just a surprise."

"I'm glad you don't see it as butting in." I thought I heard relief in his voice.

"Of course I don't. But tell me, what did you find out?"

"Next to nothing, I'm afraid. I would have called you immediately if I had. I talked to a man who remembered a car-train accident, but my leads, which were a scant few anyway, turned out to be dead ends. I have another avenue to pursue, but I can do that from Cairo."

"Maybe we can find out where Jeffrey is buried."

"Maybe," he told me. "Would that make you feel better?"

"Yes, I think so," I told him, "but promise me you won't neglect your work."

"I won't," he assured me.

The conversation was winding down. Neither of us seemed ready to broach the topic of the other night. I thanked him again for the Nightingale book, which I'd mentioned earlier in our call, and then he told me he would see me in a couple of days.

"I'll call you if I hear something before then," he added. "Have fun seeing the sights and with Lauren. And Lissa?"

"Yes?"

"Pleasant dreams."

"And the same to you, Steve. Thanks for calling."

CHAPTER ELEVEN

After breakfast the next morning, from the hotel dining room's buffet, I was on my way back to my room when I passed the jewelry shop just off the lobby and an attractively arranged window caught my eye. In spite of my mistake with Asmie, the fact remained that gold was a good buy in Egypt. It seemed as good a time as any to begin looking in earnest for gifts to take home, and I knew from Aunt Miriam that, unlike Asmie's and many places in the bazaars, this particular shop was reputable.

I enjoyed browsing when the unobtrusive salesman didn't pounce upon me. What a captivating array of jewelry I saw within the glass display cases. There were collars reminiscent of Cleopatra and Nefertiti, with real lapis and carnelian and other semi-precious gems, scarabs in gold or inlaid with jewels, and a wide assortment of amulets. And wouldn't it be nice, I thought, if one could wear an *ankh* to actually bring good fortune and a long life, or a stylized eye-shaped *udjat* to ward off snakebite, illness, and curses?

I gravitated toward a display case filled with cartouches and asked to see several trays, which soon revealed quality workmanship surpassing even that of Asmie's heavy gold *bait* cartouche, usually in 18-karat gold as charms or rings. Like the ones in Asmie's store, some were replicas of actual pharaonic seals—I recognized those of Seti I and Akhenaten, to name but two—and others were blank for personalization with modern names.

I ordered two of the latter, for my mother and my sister-in-law, as well as a miniaturized version for Tracy, but I'd given up on the idea of a cartouche for my friend since these were more than I wanted to pay for her souvenir. When the jeweler told me I could pick them up sometime after four o'clock the day after tomorrow, I was especially pleased that I'd stepped into the store.

As I was about to leave, I thought to ask the salesman, who I'd learned was also the proprietor, if he knew of somewhere I might take the Bastet to be repaired. For some reason, having it in two pieces bothered me. Luck was with me. After examining the damage to the stone cat, the man told me he could have it done for me and ready to pick up with the cartouches.

Three large tour groups were flooding into Karnak across the footbridge as I arrived, and although at first I melted into the crowd and would have crossed the bridge, I veered away at the last minute, deciding I would rather enter at my own speed a bit later. When I noticed even more tourists alighting from large tour buses in a nearby parking lot, I was glad I had waited.

To give them time to enter and disperse within the massive complex, I killed time by walking over to a small, lone shop just outside the temple grounds that had caught my eye on my earlier trip to Karnak because it featured rows of Bastets in its windows. As I neared the tiny shop, I saw gray cats, blue cats, green cats—a rainbow of colors, in several sizes. How enchanting!

A toothy Egyptian around my age greeted me in Arabic as I entered and began looking around, and the hard-sell I was beginning to expect at any but the best stores came as the gung-ho salesman scribbled prices in Egyptian pounds as fast as I looked closely at individual statuettes.

"Jade," he said as I glanced at a green one.

Fat chance, I thought, as he handed it to me. It was stately and beautiful, with a lovely smoothness to it, but when the man turned to pull still another Bastet from the shelf and I surreptitiously scratched its base lightly with my thumbnail, I knew the telltale mark meant it was probably only soapstone and not even remotely as valuable as jade. It was a pretty souvenir priced as a true objet d'art. I shook my head.

A blue cat, also soapstone, that resembled Aunt Miriam's gift, only lighter in color, drew my attention.

"Soapstone," I enunciated carefully as I held the noble little cat to inspect it for chips. I quoted a price and bargained a bit and soon had the purchase tucked inside my bag.

By the time I crossed the footbridge, Karnak had swallowed up the crowds, and with no one standing in the Avenue of Rams, I took several pictures. Again, I had the sensation of vastness as I looked between the towers of the First Pylon, down the length of this awesome remnant of the past.

For the next three hours, I was lost in a veritable wonderland of temples, columns, and magnificent statuary and reliefs that told ancient stories such as that of Rameses II smiting his foes before Amun. Symbols abounded everywhere. In the First Hall of Records, for instance, prominent were two granite pillars, one with the lotus to denote Upper Egypt and the other bearing papyrus to represent Lower Egypt. Additional testimony to the unified realm of the. pharaohs appeared within cartouches and on grand reliefs time and again in the double crown, the *pschent*, worn by the rulers of the united kingdom.

I didn't know whether to laugh or cry when I spotted two towering statues of Rameses II, whose wife, Nefertari, stood revealingly miniaturized in front of his legs.

Snapping pictures and consulting my guidebook as I went along, I again came to the Temple of Amun and at one point thought of Lauren, who no doubt would be offended by evidence that here, too, Queen Hatshepsut's memory apparently had been sullied. Her contributions to the revamping and glorification of Karnak, a project begun when her father had made Thebes the capital of the New Kingdom and decided the older temple was much too modest, included a shrine and obelisks in her father's court. After Hatshepsut's reign had ended, though, following true to form, her stepson pulled down many of her improvements or rebuilt to hide such features as her obelisks from view.

Amun was alive and well at Karnak if the sun's intensity was any indication. It was getting hot, and I was glad I'd worn my hat and a loose-fitting blouse with my culottes.

As I made my way back to the Sacred Lake, this time I felt better and noticed more. Especially catching my fancy was a giant granite scarab beetle. A symbol of the rising sun, scarabs bearing a portion of the *Book of the Dead* on their bellies, I remembered, had been placed on mummies in the position of the deceased's heart. I had seen several of the beetles carved into reliefs on Karnak's walls and obelisks, but this three-dimensional figure, though outsized, looked far more real.

Even though this time I carried a small bottle of water with me, I ordered a soft drink at the refreshment stand and sipped it at a table in the shaded area beside the lake after purchasing some postcards. I dashed off a couple of greetings and then decided to have a second look at the stone cat I'd bought earlier, which I dubbed Bastet II.

It was admittedly only the stuff of souvenirs, but its lines, demeanor, and hieroglyphic good-luck inscription were attractive. The little statue would make an interesting addition to my friend Lori's cat collection. I noticed that the blue of the soapstone had a slightly smoky cast to it that Aunt Miriam's cat—Bastet I—did not with its dark blue veining have, and again I wondered how fine a piece Bastet I was. I supposed I could ask the hotel jeweler for an appraisal, but then again, maybe it was none of my business.

As I returned Bastet II to my bag and finished my drink, I grew enthusiastic at the thought of getting a more detailed look at the Great Hypostyle Hall, which I knew was the largest single chamber of any temple in the world.

And what a phenomenon it was! With 134 massive inscribed columns in sixteen rows dwarfing me, I felt almost as if I were standing within a reddish-brown stone woods. To Steve, it had seemed like a redwood forest. The twelve largest columns flanking the hall's central aisle soared sixty-nine feet high and had a girth of more than thirty-three feet, topped by open-flower, eleven-foot-high capitals so enormous that each stone flower was reputed to have room for about 100 persons to stand. Although the 122 other columns, with closed-bud capitals, were smaller, they were no less impressive in their sheer number. The columns had had to be solid and numerous to support a stone roof covering an area larger than a football field.

Thoroughly fascinated by the now-roofless architectural wonder, I walked through the "forest" at leisure. Quite a distance from the hall's central aisle, where few other tourists had strayed on this hot afternoon, I came to some fine reliefs of Seti I on the north side. I saw Seti's inscribed likeness offering incense before entering the temple and kneeling before Amun and Khons as he received symbols of a long reign.

Near the reliefs, in the spirit of exploring every nook and cranny, I happened to enter an alcove about six-feet-by-three-feet in size. Wondering what it had been for, I stepped into the low-ceilinged little room to see if it led anywhere, and felt the temperature drop significantly. There were walls on two sides, but on the third, to my left, closing the little room off, were iron bars that blocked access to a dim flight of thirty to forty dangerously sloping stairs littered with bricks and other debris. "Spooky," Lauren would call it, I thought with a smile.

Just for the sake of curiosity, I whipped out the _Baedecker's_ from my tote bag to check the diagram of the Great Hypostyle Hall to try to determine where the ascending steps led. There were so many stairs that I thought it might be to a pylon or the enclosure wall.

To have enough light to read, I moved a bit closer to the alcove's opening and had just begun to intently peruse the appropriate page when, though I'd seen and heard no one, suddenly I felt a hard tug at my shoulder, followed by a violent shove that sent me sprawling.

The guidebook flew out of my hands as I used them to break my fall, and fortunately, although I did scrape my hands and bang one knee as I went down, I was more shaken up than hurt.

There was a casualty of another type, however. My tote bag was gone.

Even though I was back on my feet immediately, the thief had disappeared within the forest of columns, which this far from the hall's central passage did not feature any tourists at the moment. As dismayed as I was, I counted myself lucky. I wasn't badly hurt, and although I'd lost my flashlight, bottled water and Bastet II, along with a few other items, fortunately my valuables were in the purse fastened around my waist; my camera had been around my neck. I was also relieved that I had been holding the guidebook Aunt Miriam had given me for high school graduation, or it would have disappeared with my bag.

Suddenly, I wanted to be out from within the shadowy columns, in sunlight among the crowds I often shunned.

As I walked through the hotel lobby after my return, I heard a voice hail me with, "Oh, Lissa, I'm glad I caught up with you."

"Hello, Mrs. Brenner," I said to the woman who was rapidly approaching me. I looked for Lauren but did not see her.

She must have noticed my scraped hands and dirtied knee. "You're hurt!"

"A little," I told her, explaining that I had taken a tumble at Karnak. She advised me to put some antiseptic on my scratches.

"Do you have time to walk over there and talk for a few minutes?" she asked as she pointed to a quiet area of the lobby not far from the jewelry shop.

"I'd love to," I said. As we made our way there, I told

her I hoped her husband was feeling better.

"Thank you, he is, and I'm sure that rascal will wear his hat from now on and use sunblock." I was to learn that "that rascal" was an endearment Mrs. Brenner frequently used to describe her husband.

"Sunburn can really dampen a trip," I commented as we took identical overstuffed chairs separated by a small rattan table.

Her eyes met mine and turned serious when she said, "You've been good for Lauren, Lissa. I don't know how you did it, but she's more relaxed."

I thought she might be overemphasizing my role in any change for the better in her granddaughter, so I replied, "That's wonderful, Mrs. Brenner, but it's worked both ways. I've thoroughly enjoyed my time with Lauren. In fact, I've missed her today."

"Please call me Katherine. *Mrs. Brenner* makes me feel ancient, and although some days I feel ninety, I've still got a lot of zip left in me," she said as we exchanged smiles. She seemed so warm and down-to-earth, and the first-name basis, despite the difference in our ages, seemed appropriate, especially since I had quickly grown fond of her granddaughter.

"I'd be happy to, Katherine."

"Lauren is with Ed. She felt so sorry for him because he had to stay in and miss the Valley of the Kings, which is at the very top of his list of things to see here. Now that he's feeling chipper again, she's squiring him around the town. No doubt they're in search of donkeys to feed and a bargain or two at the bazaar."

"I hope they're having fun."

She nodded as her expression again grew more serious. I could tell that she was getting to the nitty-gritty of our conversation.

"You know, Lissa, I can tell that Lauren likes Egypt, but she's been a tense, sometimes sad little girl, as I think you probably noticed. For one thing, it's broken my heart to repeatedly hear her say in her bedtime prayers, '. . . and forgive me, please, for being so bad.' I've tried and tried to draw her out, Lissa, and just haven't gotten very far. That's where you enter the picture. Last night, Lauren skipped that portion of her prayers for the first time on this trip."

"That's wonderful," I told Lauren's grandmother. Happy that the little girl was less preoccupied, and glad for any help I might have been, I didn't want, either, to be cast in the role of miracle worker. Afraid that Katherine might be expecting too much too soon—for grief is surely an ongoing process that does not lift in one decisive motion but, rather, by degrees—I said, "I've seen the tension you mentioned."

Then I stopped momentarily, trying to decide how much to say. Although of course I wanted an honest conversation with Katherine, and to be helpful, I didn't want to betray the little girl's confidence and risk alienating her at such a fragile juncture in her life. I decided that I didn't need to get into the area of Lauren's guilt feelings.

"Lauren told me her baby brother died suddenly," I said as Katherine nodded. "I'm so sorry about that and know it must be painful for the whole family. I think it's been harder on Lauren than it may appear, generating feelings of loneliness and maybe even rejection. Katherine, she mentioned thinking that her parents sent her away to Egypt because they no longer love her."

"Rejected? The poor child!" her grandmother said with a look of stricken enlightenment. "Now I understand why she hasn't wanted to call home. Why, every time the mention of home comes up, that guarded look veils Lauren's face. I never guessed that it went beyond missing the baby.

She thinks they sent her away?"

"Yes," I said as I nodded sympathetically. This was obviously a revelation to the little girl's grandmother.

"I guess my son and daughter-in-law have focused upon their loss, Lissa, but they love that little girl very, very much. They never dreamed that by sending her to Egypt with us, Lauren might take the whole idea of being away from home right now as rejection on their parts. Maybe Ed and I have even seemed like part of the *punishment*. Lissa," she said, reaching over and touching my forearm for emphasis, "I'll tell you one thing for sure, and that's that we Brenners will do some serious communicating to get this straight once and for all. I guess we've underestimated the complexity of a child's grief. How can I ever thank you?"

"A happier Lauren is all I want, Katherine. Believe it or not, she's helped me as much as I seem to have helped her," I said as I told her that I, too, had lost someone not too long ago and was still working out my emotions.

The conversation wound down with Katherine's reminder to me to put something on my cuts, and as we were parting, she invited me to attend the Sound and Light show at Karnak with the three of them the following night.

Exhausted from my eventful afternoon at Karnak, I had a sandwich in my room and then took a nap.

When I awakened, the sun was getting low, and as I looked off my balcony, I noticed Lauren's grandfather sitting in a poolside chair. Although the chlorinated water would probably make my scrapes smart, I decided to join this third member of the Brenner triad. I liked his wife and granddaughter. The sunset, in any case, would no doubt be spectacular from the pool, which overlooked the Nile and, beyond, the looming mass of the Necropolis of Thebes.

I changed into my swimsuit and cover-up and made

my way to the empty pool.

Mr. Brenner, who was still in his chair by the shallow end, still looked red.

"Hello," I told him. "How are you this evening?"

"Hi. With the sun going down, I can finally swim," he grumbled with a wink. "The water's going to be murder when it touches this skin, though. It's still awfully raw."

"You have my condolences on the sunburn. I have to baby my skin or I end up like you did, Mr. Brenner."

"Ed."

"Would you like to try my number 50 sunblock, Ed?" I asked as I slipped into the shallow end and felt in initial stinging sensation where the chlorine hit my abrasions.

"Fifty?" he asked with amazement. "I didn't know they made one that strong. Okay, I'll slather some on for the Valley of the Kings

"Remind me to get it from my room," I said, also suggesting that just to be on the safe side, he wear a breathable shirt that covered his arms.

"Will do."

He inched into the water, wincing as the chlorine seared each new patch of burned epidermis. My stinging had subsided, fortunately, and the water felt relaxing.

"I think I'll just stand here for a minute," he commented, and since I was already just standing in the water, I stayed where I was, happily kicking my legs a little.

We exchanged tidbits about our careers—he was a retired sales representative for a large brewery in St. Louis— and then I said, "You'll find the Necropolis of Thebes impressive, and Lauren should be a great tour guide. She was an enthusiastic companion for me. Is Katherine going with you?"

"You were great to take Lauren with you, Lissa.

She hasn't stopped talking about your day there. As for Katherine, no, she's not going. She doesn't like people to know, but she tried a tomb out at Saqqara before we came here and panicked. She's had claustrophobia for as long as I've known her and won't even take an elevator unless she must.

She'd rather walk up fifty flights," he told me without any belittlement in his voice.

"She's in good company. I've noticed tourists backing out at the last minute or emerging white-faced from several tombs."

"Might be the mummies with some of them," he commented jokingly. "To some, Boris Karloff's version still walks."

I smiled at his reference to the old "Mummy" movies I'd adored as a child.

"Kath likes some time to herself now and then anyway," he remarked as he was cut off by his granddaughter.

"I'm back," Lauren trilled as she remembered just in time to slow to a walk near the pool. "Hi, Lissa. Watch this," she called just before her cannonball generously sprayed her grandfather and me. Enjoying her exuberance, we praised her frequently during her exhibition of jumps and dives.

Ed swam several laps while the little girl and I stood in the shallow end and took turns swimming between each other's legs. Then I had my swim.

As we tired and emerged from the pool to towel ourselves dry, the cliff area across the Nile that marked the legendary tombs was a black silhouette framed against the orange glow of the sky. Although much different in appearance from the sunset behind the Pyramids of Giza, the postcard-pretty scene reminded me of those moments of perfect peace with Steve.

"Sunset on the Nile," Ed Brenner commented in an awestruck tone.

"It's beautiful," I agreed.

"I love the colors," Lauren put in. Then as her grandfather walked around to the other side of the pool to retrieve his beach jacket, she added in a whisper meant just for me, "I think Jason is over there somewhere."

As I watched the child gazing intently at the ancient cemetery and the even older solar disc, I could believe it, too, and nodded wordlessly.

"And your husband," she added.

"And Jeffrey."

CHAPTER TWELVE

The man was chasing me through the countless passages and chambers of a tomb that seemed to stretch on forever. Torches illuminated my way, casting an eerie flickering light onto rock-hewn walls that were decorated with hieroglyphic texts I could not decipher and figures of gods and humans highlighted in faded ochre, carmine, olive, cobalt, and a dazzling white. I was vaguely aware that they depicted someone's life and death, but I dared not slow my pace to really take them in.

As my legs pumped furiously to get beyond the grasp of my pursuer, I looked back for a second and saw to my horror that his entire face was swathed in bandages. A strip of white cloth trailed to the ground like a streamer from a hand where one sleeve of his baggy brown suit ended.

Hurry! I told myself.

The pictorial stories on the walls became only a blur of color as I ran for my life.

Then abruptly I had come to the end of a long passageway leading into a chamber that, to my distress, was filled to overflowing with a hodgepodge of treasure that blocked my way. Trapped, I could only stare dumbly at the barrier. Hadn't

I seen that golden throne somewhere? A canopic jar at my feet also looked familiar. How I yearned to pore over every piece before me, but I knew instinctively that my life depended upon not giving in to that luxury.

Although the mummy behind me made no sound as he came, the floor vibrated ominously with each bandaged footfall, and even though he dragged one leg, somehow he was gaining on me. I had to get past the barrier.

Just then, I heard someone say my name from behind the pile of grave goods.

Help me! I screamed as no sound emerged from my lips. Behind me, the floor lurched violently as the creature closed in.

Desperately, I reached for a blue and gold staff from within the pile of gleaming objects, pulled it out, and held it before me. Like a key opening a door, the gesture parted the heap of goods just long enough for me to slip through. Then the mass of treasure closed again before the mummy could follow, and the vibrations of his footfalls ceased.

As I inhaled the heady scent of incense, I saw that the room before me was magnificent. A gilded frieze of cobras adorned the walls where they met the roof of the chamber, and a man sat on a throne.

The jackal-headed Anubis took my hand and led me to Osiris, whom I recognized from his white crown with a double feather. He held a flail and a crook.

"Welcome," he told me, and I fainted as I saw that Osiris's face looked just like Jeffrey's.

My heart was still pounding as I awakened. I'd had a nightmare something about a mummy. It must have been that reference of Ed Brenner's to mummies last evening, I told myself, glad to be in a modern hotel room on the east, living, side of the Nile just then, with a whole day stretching before me.

The Museum of Ancient Egyptian Art and Luxor Temple were on my agenda, but since the museum did not open until four o'clock that afternoon, I decided to time my trip to the temple, which was not far from the museum, so that I could see both attractions on one trip.

Especially since my knee was a bit tender from yesterday's fall, the lull was welcome. I spent the morning quietly writing in my neglected travel journal and jotting a few more postcards. As I did, I realized how my thumbnail sketches of vacation scenes failed to touch upon such happenings as seeing a dead-ringer for my late husband, sharing some sizzling moments with my best friend, being followed by a man in a brown suit, and toting around a Bastet that turned out to have a key at its heart.

The key!

Some courier I made. Not only had I dropped the statuette, breaking it apart, but I had also left Bastet I for repair without the key for replacement into the hollowed space where it had nestled before the accident on the train. Thinking that perhaps it wasn't too late to have it sealed back inside, I dressed and returned to the shop, only to find that the proprietor wasn't working that day and his employee knew nothing about my Bastet. When he looked around the shop's back room, he found no sign of the stone cat. I would just have to hope to catch the jeweler later.

From a shop near the jeweler's, I bought a tote bag to replace the one that had been snatched at Karnak and dropped my postcards off in the lobby. When I routinely checked my box at the front desk for messages, a little to my surprise, I spotted something.

"Thank you," I told the desk clerk as I accepted a rather fat envelope and what seemed to be a piece of paper from a notepad.

On the way back down the long hallway to my room, I opened the thinner of the two communiques and felt a stab of disappointment as I read from a page emblazoned with the hotel's ram's head logo that Mr. Steven Matson would be tied up at least until Thursday and would not be able to join me in Luxor as planned.

Tied up? What on earth did that mean? He had given me no indication when we'd spoken on the phone that he might not be meeting me. In fact, when I thought of all the plans we had so enthusiastically made—seeing Seti I's tomb together, for one thing—I was puzzled.

Extra time in Luxor on my own didn't faze me in the slightest, but what had come up that was so important? Would sketching portals be that urgent? In all fairness, I supposed that someone with a fantastic door might have insisted upon a given time for an appointment and indicated loss of interest if that weren't convenient for Steve, but that didn't seem likely, for some reason.

My heart skipped a beat as another explanation for his change of plans crossed my mind. Had Steve taken off again for Turkey?

On the phone, that possibility hadn't come up, and now when I thought of it, the idea that Steve might have returned to the land where Jeffrey had died was unsettling.

Because I was sure I wouldn't rest easily until I knew more, for the time being I ignored the second piece of correspondence in my hand and hurriedly unlocked my door. Then I tried putting through a call to Steve in Cairo. I listened futilely, however, as his phone rang unanswered.

As I hung up and walked over to the window that faced the Valley of the Kings, a third possibility stung me.

Maybe Steve just didn't want to see me. Was I only like a sister to him after all? The thought that perhaps we had ruined a beautiful friendship the other night at the Mena House, compromising its integrity, made me feel sick. "What have we done, Steve?" my heart implored as I stood that way for several minutes, seeing a procession of images that spanned all the years of our friendship—all the sharing, the mutual support, the caring—rather than the vista in the line of my gaze.

I finally opened the second, heavier message, which turned out to be a note from Katherine Brenner. When I pulled the single sheet of stationery from the envelope, irritation prickled as an Egyptian Air ticket fluttered to the floor. I didn't want to be manipulated, and a paid ticket with my name on it fell into that category. A bit miffed, I left the ticket on the floor as I unfolded Katherine's note, which read:

Dear Lissa:

Come with us to Aswan and Abu Simbel. It's only for three days, and we'll give you plenty of time to sightsee on your own. Forgive me for being highhanded. I just feel that Lauren isn't quite ready to say goodbye to you. Please think it over and let us know.

Katherine B.

Highhanded it was, but the odd thing is that after reading Katherine's message, I realized that I wasn't quite ready to say goodbye to Lauren, either. The little girl and I had begun something mutually beneficial by way of our curiously intersecting grief processes. Although three extra days together wouldn't necessarily add much to our insight or respective healing, Lauren and I could still cement a rather unique friendship that somehow seemed meant to be.

Since Steve would not be joining me on schedule, there was no reason not to go. I would insist, however, upon paying my own way.

We took gharries—Lauren and I in one horse-drawn carriage and her grandparents in another to Karnak just before dark that night. We didn't need our hats or sunblock this time, but we'd brought along insect repellant and lightweight jackets, since sundown on the fringe of the desert can bring marked coolness.

"Clop, clop," sang the child as our horse moved us along at a slow, steady pace.

"It's a nice sound, isn't it?"

"Mmm-hmm."

Lauren's eyes sparkled and reminded me again of delphiniums. "Guess what?" she invited.

"What?"

"Mom and Daddy called the hotel last night, *just to talk to me,* and they said they miss me so much and can hardly wait for me to come back. Mom and I are going to put up new wallpaper in my room, and Daddy thinks we should get a puppy and plan a fishing trip. They love me, Lissa!"

I hugged the little girl, so happy for her. I knew the adjustment wasn't over, but the family had taken a step in the right direction.

"Of course they do, sweetheart."

I learned later that Mrs. Brenner had phoned Lauren's parents and chewed them out lovingly but firmly about needing to demonstrate their love for the child who was alive, and that had resulted in the phone call that had so lifted Lauren's spirits.

Now it was my turn to surprise the little girl. "Guess what?" I queried.

"You're funny," Lauren told me as we drew nearer to Karnak.

"I know, but you're supposed to ask me what."

"Okay. What?"

"I'm going to Aswan and Abu Simbel with you."

I had spoken to Katherine and Ed at the hotel after their return from the Valley of the Kings to make sure they really wanted me along. They did, and we had agreed that Lauren would hear the news from me. "She'll be so happy, Lissa," Katherine had told me, mentioning that although their day at the Necropolis of Thebes had been enjoyable, Lauren had gotten mopey at times at the thought of the Sound and Light show being our last time together.

Katherine had assessed her granddaughter correctly. Now on the way to Karnak, I had to caution Lauren not to fall as she spontaneously tried to jump up and down in delight in our gharry.

A great many tourists had gathered near the First Pylon for the Sound and Light spectacular, which began as a walking tour at the Avenue of Rams. While spotlights played dramatically over selected features of Karnak as the mass of humanity moved along, narrator highlighted historical, mythological and architectural aspects of the great complex in a way that almost magically transported the sensitive, including my young friend, I was happy to note, into a past when white-robed priests had strolled the great halls and glittering jubilees had occurred.

Our short stature was less a disadvantage than I had expected. Lost as we were among people much taller, Lauren and I, although we missed the lights on some of the reliefs, for instance, had only to look up as Karnak's huge scale afforded us the reward of an inscribed obelisk here or a lotus capital there. Still, I was glad to have first seen Karnak by daylight.

I had seen the Son et Lumiere show at the Acropolis of Athens, which had certainly grabbed my spirit, but Karnak's was different in that the Egyptians had preserved their rulers as mummies and in detailed hieroglyphic texts, and given them faces via their tomb and other art. Seti I, Rameses II, the Ptolemies—the individuals within their historical framework came alive in a unique way.

As we strolled past the Sacred Lake near the Temple of Amun on our way to bleachers for the latter part of the show, Lauren tugged at my elbow, pointed to the giant scarab that had also caught my fancy, and said, "That's my favorite thing here." Her grandparents smiled at our rapport when I agreed how special I also thought the sacred beetle was.

The bleachers, I was pleased to note, were unobtrusively to one side of Karnak's major points of interest, to the east of the Sacred Lake. As we sat down and looked out over the lake, lights continued to pinpoint the many pylons and other features as the narrator furthered such images as sacred barques of the Amun/Mut/Khans Triad flowing here in the Festival of Opet at flood time.

"This is wonderful," Katherine commented. "I can almost see the statues of the gods on the canopies of the boats."

Lauren, meanwhile, was pleased to hear that the Eighth Pylon was Hatshepsut's.

"They didn't knock it down," she said of the substantially large double towers. "I'm glad." I was, too, and didn't spoil the little girl's satisfaction by telling her that the Queen's names had been erased.

Just for a moment, when the spotlights played over the part of the Temple Precinct where I had been pushed and my bag stolen, I recalled the brief moment of terror the day before and felt a shiver course down my spine. As the bright lights accentuated the inky pools of blackness that had become most of the temple area, I was glad to be among other people, especially three who had become friends.

I tried calling Steve after returning, again with no success, to let him know that soon I would be off to Nubia. Although I still felt uneasy about his sudden, sketchily explained change of plans, I also just wanted to talk, to tell him about my evening and to let him know, too, how much I appreciated his emphasis upon my visiting the museum.

A gem as museums go, it featured a tastefully displayed small collection of finds from the Thebes area that included a realistic stone image of Sobek, the crocodile god, a colossal red granite head of Amenophis III, and a gilded Hathor.

At least in discussing Egypt, I felt on firm ground with Steve.

About the rest I would just have to wait to see.

CHAPTER THIRTEEN

The side trip to Aswan and Abu Simbel turned out to be a blur of fun, good sightseeing and serious thinking, with only a couple of things—one of them quite upsetting—happening to mar my stay in Nubia.

The Brenners and I arrived in Aswan by air from Luxor the following day and proceeded to our hotel, on Elephantine Island, first by bus and then by boat. Lauren had enjoyed all the stages of the journey, whereas Katherine immediately fell in love with our hotel, enchanted as she was by its brilliant tropical flowers in beds and bougainvillea cascading over the walls as we approached the building on foot from the boat landing. Ed was thinking ahead to visiting the dam.

After checking in, we had lunch and went to our respective rooms. To my pleasure, I had a breathtaking view from my third-floor balcony. There were so many faces to Egypt. This time, instead of a pyramid or fabled necropolis, tall date palms rose gracefully on the part of the island I could see, whose tip jutted into the Nile like the prow of a ship. Perhaps reflecting the clear blue of the sky, the river shone sapphire, and I was delighted to see it dappled with *feluccas*, the snowy-sailed boats that plied the waters. Additional examples of Katherine's *tropical splendod* appeared below me in clusters of pink and red.

Although the vegetation was lush right here, however, I knew that areas surrounding Aswan were generally uncultivable. When I looked beyond the island to my left, in fact, I could see no sign of greenness on the west bank—only sand and rock stretching up and away seemingly forever in what must be the tomb area abutting the great expanse of desert. To my right, in contrast to the emptiness of the desert, was the bustling city of Aswan, whose modern high-rises I could see from my balcony aerie in the distance on the east bank.

My phone rang before I had had a chance to unpack, but I was happy to drop everything when I learned that Ed had wangled us seats on a felucca for a ride that very afternoon. I hurriedly changed from a skirt into lightweight slacks and rubber soled shoes.

What a joy it was to finally sail on the Nile. *The Nile!* I thought with a tremor of excitement.

"I feel like pinching myself, too," Ed remarked.

The sturdy sailboat, with ten aboard, sat low in the water and moved along at a steady clip, thanks to the skills of our Nubian skipper and his crew of one. Clad in galabias and barefoot, both young men exhibited a certain joie de vivre that was infectious.

"Those rocks look like elephants taking a bath," Lauren said at one point in reference to the many granite projectiles in the water not far below the First Cataract.

"Elephant Land," commented a woman passenger who had overheard the child. About sixty, she seemed to be with two other women. The trio leaned closer to us as the first woman explained, "This was once called *Yebu*, or *Elephant Land*, maybe because the people long ago thought these rocks looked like elephants. Or there may once have been herds of real elephants spotted here."

"Is that how our island got its name?" Lauren asked the woman.

"It is, and you are a perceptive little girl."

Lauren turned rather shy then, and the conversation died comfortably as we sat back and savored the view and the glorious feel of the Nubian wind on our faces. The air was warm under a clear sky, and Ed, I was happy to note, had applied liberal sunblock and wore long sleeves to guard his fair skin from the potent rays of the sun. Except for the Nubians, whose ebony skin protected them, we all wore hats to shield our faces.

Shortly before we docked at the foot of a promontory crowned by the domed Mausoleum of the Aga Khan, Katherine told me she didn't feel up to the steep climb, so I decided to let Ed and Lauren go together while I kept her company. Badway, our wiry skipper, assured us he would be happy to have us stay aboard the felucca, which suddenly was in the company of about twenty other similar vessels.

As Katherine and I waved Lauren and Ed on their way, Badway leapt off the boat to have hot tea with a couple of other skippers.

"Are you all right, Katherine?" I asked. She looked fine, but since usually she did everything that didn't entail getting into a dark, closed-in space, I was concerned.

"Oh definitely, Lissa," she reassured me, "but keeping up with a nine-year-old takes more stamina than I'd remembered, and I want to save some energy for Abu Simbel tomorrow."

"I can hardly wait to see it myself," I said of the

extraordinary monument that had been moved piece by piece to save it from being flooded with the construction of the Aswan High Dam.

"And what about you?" she asked, surprising me. "Would you like to tell me why you've looked so preoccupied lately? It isn't concern about Lauren, is it?"

"Oh no," I hurriedly replied. "In fact, I see her making great strides. The phone call from her parents was just what she needed."

"Good. So what's on your mind?" she inquired. Then with a little smile she added, "Or am I being a busybody?"

Beneath her souvenir white sailor hat that had *Luxor* stamped on it, Katherine's brown eyes glowed warmly, inviting me to talk, and suddenly for the very reason that she didn't know Steve and was not a close friend, she seemed exactly the right person to talk to.

"No, that's one thing you're not, so don't worry. It's just hard to find the words," I said, pausing as I tried to decide how much to tell her. I didn't really want to get into the strange issue of the Jeffrey look-alike or my disenchantment following his death.

Katherine tried to help me out by asking, "It's a matter of the heart, isn't it?"

"It is," I told her with a smile as I wondered if there was a universal aura one woman detects in another when it comes to romance. "Katherine, do you think it's possible to know a man, to love him platonically for many years, and then suddenly fall in love with him?"

She thought for only a moment before answering.

"I think it's the realization that's sudden, Lissa, but that the actual falling in love has happened gradually over a period of time. Some catalyst at some point in the relationship just has a way of removing the blinders, making you aware in a way you hadn't been before. To tell you the truth, I'm always skeptical when people say they've fallen in love in the blink of an eye. Attraction, yes, but real love requires getting to know a person and that takes the test of time and shared experiences. Many a relationship fizzles because *love at first sight* has only been chemistry."

I was considering her words when Badway strode purposefully back aboard the felucca, went to the stern and leaned over to bathe his hands, arms and face in the Nile. He walked back to the center of the boat, where he unselfconsciously knelt and bent down from the waist, arms stretched out front, so that his forehead touched the deck. He raised and lowered his upper body several times.

We hadn't been aware of a muezzin's call, but as Katherine and I watched the handsome young man, we realized that we were witnessing the Muslim prayer ritual, or *salat*.

After a few minutes, it was over and Badway was back on shore drinking tea with his cronies. Fascinated and touched by what had seemed like more than just rote to the Nubian, Katherine and I had remained respectfully silent through his period of prayer. Facing Mecca five times a day in prayerful supplication was no longer a stereotype to either of us, though. Badway had personalized it.

"Amazing, wasn't it?" Katherine commented after he was back on land, and as I nodded, she tried to pick up our conversation where we'd left off.

"What's this fellow's name?"

"Steve."

"What's Steve like, Lissa?"

I told her how we'd met in high school and formed a fast friendship that had continued even through my marriage to another man.

"Steve is my best friend," I summed up.

"You said that last as if it distresses you."

"Did I? Well, even though we are, I guess I'm afraid I overstepped the boundaries of that friendship and—I don't know—somehow betrayed the comfortable, almost brother/sister relationship we'd had for so long."

"Do you think it's a one-sided change, then?" she asked.

I remembered the long kiss along the highway and the mounting passion in the hotel room later.

"No, I'm pretty sure he felt something too. I guess what bothers me is not that it happened but wondering if he regrets it."

"What was the catalyst to this change in your relationship? How are things different?" she asked.

I told her about the kiss in the sunset after our relaxing day at Memphis and Saqqara when Steve and I had still been our old easy selves.

"What's the problem then? It sounds beautiful. I'll tell you something," she said, leaning closer. "Falling in love with your best friend is just about the most wonderful way love between a man and a woman can happen. Ed and I have been married for forty-six years, and he was my best friend before the wedding and has remained my best friend through thick and through thin for almost five decades. That's a lot of time—too much time!—to spend with someone who is not your best friend."

"That makes sense."

"But?"

"But he's avoiding me, Katherine."

"What makes you think so, dear?" she asked very gently. I knew my hurt and fear must be on my sleeve.

I told her about his lunch cancellation in Cairo the

day I left for Luxor and then his changing our plans to meet in Upper Egypt.

Katherine thought for a moment and then said, "Just think of the sorting out you've been doing, Lissa. Hasn't it occupied a lot of your time and thoughts?"

"It certainly has," I told her emphatically.

"Well, don't you think that maybe your Steve is also doing a lot of sorting out? He may be just as worried as you are that the romantic turn of events has ruined a friendship he treasures every bit as much as you do. Maybe he's afraid to see you, Lissa, afraid of his own desire if, by chance, you are the one who regrets those passionate kisses. Remember, in this situation which is so new to you both, he doesn't know for sure how you feel any more than you know how he feels."

That must be it, I thought, as I felt some of the lead leave my heart.

"The poor guy," I said with a lilt to my voice, "maybe he's as miserable as I am."

Katherine and I laughed at the incongruity of my words to the happy note in my voice. Then I kissed her on the cheek as I thanked her for her listening ear.

"Think nothing of it, but you'll have to let me know what develops, or I shall always wonder," she told me with a wink.

"You can be sure I will. I also want to correspond with Lauren after we're all back home. Would her parents approve?"

"I'm sure they would, and I know it would mean a lot to Lauren."

"To me also, Katherine. She's a dear little person."

We made small talk until Badway climbed back into the boat, and then we visited some with him. The majority of Nubians didn't understand or speak English, but Badway did a little. We learned that he owned the felucca, whose 25-foot mainmast supported a hand sewn flaxen sail, and that its ropes were Italian hemp. He lived in the Nubian village on Elephantine Island and dreamed of marrying, having five children, and making a pilgrimage to Mecca. He wanted to know what it was like where we lived, and I watched his eyes light up as I described some of the sailboats that sliced through the waters of the Columbia and Willamette rivers.

The sail back to our hotel included a stop at the gardens on Botanical Island, once known as Kitchener's Island, which delighted Katherine especially, and a sunset striated in violet, rose, and tangerine. As I looked from the glowing bands of color to either side of the river, I was struck again by the Nile's role as the demarcation between the land of the living and the land of the dead. To my left, lights were beginning to twinkle on in Aswan's high-rises, and I knew there were phosphate plants and other modern industries on that side. On the west bank, however, contrasting sharply to the modern city but a river's breadth away, the lifeless sands stretched far, far away.

For some reason, I was glad that our hotel was poised on an island between these two extremes.

"What a delightful afternoon," I commented as we docked and made our way up the incline to the hotel. "I'm so glad I could come with you."

"Me too," Lauren said as she skipped along the walk.

"Have dinner with us, Lissa," Ed invited.

"Oh, please!" the little girl put in. As I saw how soulful her big blue eyes looked, I guessed she might be a master of the pleading look.

Flicking her arm at them, Katherine said, "We'd love to have you, Lissa, but you do whatever you want to. This *pressure posse*, as I sometimes call these two rascals, can wear a person down."

I liked some of Katherine's figures of speech and laughingly said as I looked from Ed to Lauren, "I appreciate the efforts of you posse members to round me up, but I think this is one pardner who could use an early night." Then to all three of them I added, "I think I'll just order something light from room service and take a long bath."

Lauren screwed up her face but did not make a verbal protest. "We do have to rise and shine early tomorrow for Abu Simbel," Ed reminded her.

"Let's make it an early breakfast together," I suggested, watching Lauren perk up as I spoke. We settled on a rendezvous time as we walked through the lobby on our way to the elevators.

Ed and Lauren went off to one of the shops in the arcade for a roll of film while Katherine waited with me in front of the bas-relief golden wall plaque—a modern version of an ancient relief by the bank of elevators.

"I really appreciate our talk this afternoon," I told the older woman.

"Good. Things will work out." she told me reassuringly.

"I hope so. I think I'll give Steve a call this evening," I said.

"A good plan. I had a hunch you might want to," she told me with a wink just as the elevator arrived.

As it turned out, although the meal from room service was a success, the phone call to Steve was not. No one answered.

The Aswan Airport was an absolute madhouse the following morning. Every seat was taken in the lounge, and people stood body-to-body like sardines in a can, holding colorful boarding passes that did not feature seat assignments.

In such a crowd, it was amazing that a man in a brown suit caught my attention. Could it be the Brown Suit? Since he was there one moment and gone the next, apparently having melted into the crowd, I wasn't sure.

When we finally boarded and passengers literally ran to the plane and scrabbled for seats, I did not see anyone in a brown suit, at any rate. Whether or not the plane was overbooked, we didn't have a prayer of sitting together. Even Lauren was stuck next to a stranger, though she did land a coveted window seat, which meant that she might be treated to a glimpse of Abu Simbel from the air.

Had I really seen Brown Suit amidst the throngs at the airport? The question nettled during the half-hour flight, but as we landed, my excitement blotted out all thoughts of the man.

We were only twenty-five miles or so from the Sudanese border, rather in the middle of nowhere, and I wondered, as countless others no doubt have, what inspired Rameses II to build such a magnificent monument in such an isolated region. This particular spot, of course, was not quite the original, since Abu Simbel had been painstakingly moved in gigantic sections to save the temples from the rising waters of Lake Nasser. *Thank you,* I mentally told them all. What a loss if such a masterpiece had disappeared forever.

A bus met our plane at the tiny Abu Simbel Airport, near the village of New Abu Simbel, which sprang up after the temples were moved in the 1960s. As we rode along, a guide explained how the monument, built to mark Rameses II's thirtieth jubilee, had been buried by sand for centuries and had not been unearthed until the early nineteenth century, by the Swiss explorer Johann Burckhardt, who had noticed what looked like mammoth heads peeking through the sand. How exciting that must have been! A little later, Giambattista Belzoni conducted a systematic excavation.

After the bus deposited us on a windy promontory, we walked along a dusty trail, with blue water sparkling far below. Since we didn't see any evidence of the temples on our approach, it was with awe that we rounded a bend and suddenly beheld the first colossal statue of Rameses II.

How proud and utterly kingly he looked, even in profile, as he sat on his throne.

"He's so big!" Lauren exclaimed of the sculpture in the round.

As we continued around the bend, three more enormous stone forms slowly revealed themselves, until finally we faced all four of the colossal statues.

"Stupendous," Ed remarked as Katherine stood with her mouth open, while I felt a welling in my eyes.

The matching sixty-five-foot statues representing the deified Rameses II sat timelessly tranquil, wearing the royal head cloth, double crown, uraeus and stylized beard of the pharaohs.

"Oh, that one doesn't have a head," Lauren said of the second figure from the left.

"It's there at his feet," Katherine told her granddaughter as the broken colossus brought the poem "Ozymandias" to mind.

"Did they drop it when they moved the temple?" the little girl asked.

"No, honey," Ed told her. "Something, maybe an earthquake, knocked it off long, long ago, and the movers put everything back just the way they found it."

And what a job that must have been. I had read

somewhere that the large temple before us had been sawn into over 800 blocks weighing twenty tons apiece and then meticulously reconstructed. Why, I could hardly notice the seams, and the temple looked as if it had always been in just that spot.

After we had visually examined the four countenances of the Pharaoh, details began to jump out. The larger than life-sized figures of women, one of whom I knew was Rameses II's second wife, Nefertari, stood dwarfed near the Pharaoh's legs. The facade of the temple behind the four colossi was trapezoidal and featured a frieze of baboons, cartouches, a band of serpents, and inscriptions dedicating the temple to Amun-re and Re-Harakhty.

As the wind whipped our hair, we stood and stared for some time before entering the temple between two of the statues, where a guard with a gigantic *ankh* key stood. Inside, we were treated to still more huge statues, reliefs of great battle scenes, and a sanctuary where on only two days out of each year the sun streams in to illuminate the venerated visages.

The smaller of the two rock temples, dedicated to Hathor and Nefertari, caught Lauren's fancy with its Hathor-headed pillars.

"Cow's ears. I remember them from Deir el-Bahri," she explained. If she decided not to be a nurse and ever became an Egyptologist, I thought fondly, no doubt she would devote herself to Hatshepsut and Deir el-Bahri.

Again, we happily explored nooks and crannies. "Where's Katherine?" I asked at one point.

"Out in the open, no doubt," Ed told me. I hadn't thought of the temple as particularly closed-in, but perhaps to a claustrophobic it might seem a little dark.

"You two keep looking around, I'll go find Katherine," I offered. Lauren seemed content to stay with her grandfather, who was discussing Hathor with her as I left.

I found Katherine savoring the sunshine and wind, even though it seemed a bit chilly to me.

"Hi, Lissa," she said as I approached. "Isn't this a wonderful spot?"

"It certainly is. I missed you in there, though."

"Did they tell you what happened after you went to your room last night?"

"Why no. Tell me."

No wonder she'd been wary today of entering anything that even faintly resembled a closed space, for after I'd gone to my room and her family returned with their newly purchased film, Katherine had decided to brave the elevator with them and had gotten stuck between floors.

"It was a nightmare for me, made worse by a wise guy yelling, *I want my mummy. I want my mummy.* No one came to our rescue for the longest time, Lissa, even though many of us were pounding like mad to get some attention. It turned out that an engineer had heeded the alarm and was working on getting the elevator moving again, but I was simply petrified—felt like I was smothering in there. Someone finally pried the doors apart, and we had to worm our way through a foot-high space."

"How terrible for you, Katherine," I told her with feeling. A nightmare it must have been.

"I'm a ninny, I guess," she told me, obviously ashamed of her fear.

"No, you're not. Most of us have at least one intense fear. Mine is of rats. I can't tell you why, either, but the thought of them gives me the absolute willies. So if you're a ninny, you're in the company of another one."

We laughed at our fears, though not at each other.

"Those rascals aren't keeping you from seeing all you want, are they?" she asked, changing the subject.

"No, not at all. I've basked in all the details my mind can process for now, and it's pretty nice to be able to come outdoors and sit here and just soak in the overall impact of Abu Simbel. I can't believe I'm really seeing these temples. Pinch me."

Katherine playfully tweaked my arm just as Ed and Lauren came out of the small temple.

"What are you doing, Grandma?"

"Pinching our friend," she said matter-of-factly as we two grown-up girls began giggling.

Looking at his watch, Ed approached us and said, "Come on, you giggle-pusses, we'd best start the walk back up to the bus for the ride back to the airport."

"Giggle-pusses," Lauren repeated as, laughing herself, she took Katherine by one hand and me by the other.

As we passed the four colossal figures of Rameses II at the large temple once again, the laughter was a sun of sorts that, unknown to me, was to set prematurely that afternoon.

CHAPTER FOURTEEN

"I want to look like one of those women," Lauren pronounced of locals in traditional dress as we strolled the alleys of Aswan's open-air bazaar district that afternoon. Not as large or as notorious as Cairo's Khan el-Khalili, this bazaar featured a wide variety of goods, including some finds amidst a welter of baubles and downright junk. The conglomeration delighted the nine-year-old child.

"Okay, Lauren, let's see if we can find something in your size," I told her. Ed, who had returned to Botanical Island with Katherine that afternoon, had given us money for an outfit for his granddaughter, and I was caught up in the little girl's glee as she flitted from one beaded scarf and colorful piece of clothing striated to another.

As we passed the myriad stalls. I noticed that exotic spices were especially popular here, and had not I been advised that trying to get them through Customs when reentering the United States could be hit or miss, I think I would have purchased a fistful of bags containing special seasonings for my own *tahina* sauce and other Eastern delicacies I planned to try making at home.

I was glad I'd worn my waist-purse instead of carrying

the easily snatchable shoulder bag I normally preferred using, since there was a lot of jostling and being ogled at by the vendors and other shoppers, who were predominantly locals. The sight of women shoppers with baskets on their heads, the sound of strangely-cadenced Arabic voices, the mingled odors of searing lamb and incense, and the feel of new fabrics and inlaid boxes—the overall strangeness of the sights, sounds, scents and tactile sensations—made me feel a little like having fallen into a James Bond movie. It was very foreign, somehow exotic, and slightly sinister.

"There!" Lauren exclaimed as she pointed to a vending stall with its selection of clothing displayed far from elegantly. Featured garments, highlighted as they were full-length against a backdrop of the stall's three canvas *walls*, reminded me of tapestries decorating real walls. If their smudges were any indication, a few of them had obviously been on display for a long while. Since so many of the stands we had already passed lacked anything in Lauren's size, I was relieved to see that some of these were scaled for the small woman or child.

"Which one?" I asked Lauren as we stepped closer.

"You buy," the tea-colored vendor said as we approached. His mouth curved into a smile, revealing several missing teeth. He no doubt felt a sale coming on.

"We buy . . . maybe," I told him, not wanting to seem so eager that we couldn't bargain down to a fair price. He had already scooped an armful of garments off a table and held them out, but Lauren already knew what she wanted.

"That black one, Lissa," she told me sotto voce.

"It's beautiful," I told her, "but are you sure you want the black?"

She nodded, and I could understand her preference since many of the women we'd seen wore black. This was no ordinary going-to-market dress, though, bedecked as it was down its bodice and long sleeves with gold beads. When I pointed to it, the man brought it closer so that we could examine it. The fabric wasn't really all that good on close inspection, but I was afraid all those hand sewn beads might still price it out of our range.

The man quoted a price in Egyptian pounds. I quoted a sum half that amount.

In what may have been only mock indignation, the vendor ranted in Arabic and then named a price about two-thirds of his original offer. I tried to bargain lower, but he wouldn't budge.

To my surprise, little Lauren, no doubt experienced from having visited bazaars in other places with her grandparents, succeeded where I had failed, ending up with complementary beaded head scarf on the house. She promptly draped it over her head theatrically, and the vendor smiled broadly at her. She didn't look even remotely Egyptian, but I could tell that she felt Egyptian, and maybe that was half the fun of dressing up. She finally removed the scarf so that it could go into a bag with the dress.

"I love it," she told me as soon as we'd bade the salesman goodbye.

"I do too," I assured her. It wasn't an outfit Lauren would wear on an American street, but it would make a memorable souvenir and might double as a costume for a party.

"Now it's your turn, Lissa," she said.

"My turn?"

"You need something Egyptian to wear, too," she said as we snaked down the merchandise-crammed alleys. Carpets, household goods, clothing galore, and jewelry vied for our attention and pounds. Lauren thought for a few moments and came up with, "I know! Lissa, you should be a belly dancer."

"I should? *Me?*"

"Yeah, you," she said, laughing. It was so good to see that sober look gone that I reveled in her gaiety. About the last thing I'd ever thought to bring home from Egypt was a belly dancing outfit, but it wouldn't hurt to look for fun.

That's how I ended up getting talked into a gaudy heliotrope sequin and chiffon creation I was sure I wouldn't be caught dead in even at a costume party. Come to think of it, though, it was actually less revealing than a swimsuit. It was Lauren who made the final color selection, which had come down to the purple or the neon green.

The fun continued, and we ended up with still another outfit, this time all in white and for Steve, just like the flowing robe and headdress worn by Peter O'Toole as Lawrence of Arabia. Also blond, Steve would look smashing.

"Whew," I finally remarked, "I'm ready to sit down and have something cool to drink. How about you?"

"Me too. Are your legs screaming?"

"*Not* this time, but my feet are tired."

"Your dogs," she said. "Mine are too."

"My dogs? Oh, my feet."

"That's what Gramps calls them."

We'd gotten quite deep into the bazaar area. Although sunset wouldn't be for quite some time, the alleyways had become shadowy as the sun lowered, and as we made our way out of the maze, I held on tightly to our packages and kept a close eye on Lauren, whose river of golden hair attracted the stares of many. When I looked around and saw no other tourists, an aura of potential intrigue permeated our carefree afternoon, and that movie set feeling was back. Lauren must have felt it, too, because she kept looking over her shoulder.

Nothing happened, however, and the feeling vanished as we reached the corniche, where shops were shops with real walls instead of mere vending stalls in alleys.

"We are certainly going to make interesting-looking Egyptians," I commented as we sipped bottled colas a little later just off a shop that fronted the Nile.

"Are you going to take belly dancing lessons now?" Lauren asked.

"I guess I'll have to, won't I?"

She nodded avidly. We fell silent then, and as we slowly drank our beverages, we looked out over the river, where we could see Elephantine Island and the tower of our hotel.

My spirits had flown high after the brief conversation with Katherine the afternoon before. Back in my room after our felucca ride, not knowing about the nightmare Katherine was facing on the stalled elevator, I had had *leban zabadi,* a thick, creamy yoghurt, in my room and then let the evening breeze caress my hair as I wondered if I had been fighting my feelings for Steve.

Now that I really thought about it, and with Katherine's words fresh in mind, I realized that "best friends" status was a solid foundation for a viable romantic love.

Jeffrey and I had been passionate lovers, but friends? In a way, of course, we were. We went places together and talked about tennis, decorating our condo, and other mundane matters, but had we ever really bared our souls to each other? He'd been so closed off. I'd seen that element to his personality before we were married—and it had bothered me a bit—but I had assured myself that once we were husband and wife, he would change and be more open. Unfortunately, it hadn't worked that way. Even though I had tried to draw Jeffrey out, he'd never been able to verbalize his deepest fears, fondest hopes and wildest dreams, and perhaps because he kept so much of himself locked away, he had never seemed interested when I had tried to voice my own.

Had our lives even intersected other than physically? I thought I'd fallen madly in love with Jeffrey at first sight, but what Katherine had said about real love needing to be based upon time and growth made sense. I realized that perhaps I'd set myself up to be bowled over by a Jeffrey. There had been Michael, after all, with whom the physical element had been so blah. When lovemaking had been wild and wonderful with Jeffrey, maybe I hadn't recognized it for what it was—mainly chemistry. Such intensity had to be real love, didn't it?

But Steve . . . Steve and I had meshed in so many important ways, intersecting feelings and ideas right and left from a time that dated all the way back to our teens. We didn't always agree, but we each knew how the other felt about issues ranging from abortion to Zen Buddhism, and we'd shared profound moments that had had nothing to do with sex and yet were almost more intimate. Whereas Jeffrey had kept his innermost feelings bottled inside himself, Steve had been open and honest with me in a way that allowed him, for example, to unabashedly cry beside me on my parents' davenport after his dog had been killed by a car, or to voice his qualms about getting into a career his dad implied was for sissies.

In turn, he had been a willing listener and frequent sympathizer whenever I had needed one.

Lauren moved slightly and returned my thoughts to Aswan. Lost in thought, as I had been, she was also staring out over the Nile. I wondered what she was seeing in her mind's eye. Ghosts, perhaps, for although we'd both made some important forward strides, we also still had more journeying before us.

"I was thinking about my little brother," she said, turning so that our eyes met.

I smiled to let her know it was a good time to talk. The soberness was back when she asked in a small voice, "Lissa, do you think Jason can see me?"

It didn't seem all that strange a question, for sometimes I wondered if, on some other plane, Jeffrey were watching me and knew what was in my heart—the disappointment, the confusion, the anger, and the ebbing love—and somehow forgave me for . . . for what? I wasn't sure, and with the expectant face of the child looking at me as if my answer were very important, it wasn't the time to try to lay any of my own old ghosts to rest. It was time to help Lauren with hers.

"I wonder, Lauren. If he can, then he knows how sorry you are that he died."

"Do you think so?"

"Oh yes, and I'll tell you something. I sometimes wonder exactly the same thing about Jeffrey, my husband."

"You do?" she asked with a certain fascination.

"I do," I told her with a little half-smile that matched her own. We were two battle-scarred soldiers finding a bit of beauty during an ongoing war.

She nodded in recognition of the mutuality of our very separate grief experiences and then said, "Sometimes it feels crummy, like I have to be super-good all the time. I mean, I'm pretty good, Lissa, but not all the time, in all the ways."

I had the sudden memory of Jeffrey complimenting me on a new dress and then spoiling it in the car halfway to a party by saying, "Oh, you wore those shoes." His tone had spoken volumes, dampening my pleasure. How often had he done that? I realized that my own self-confidence had faltered as Jeffrey's standards of perfection had begun to color my world. Sometimes now, when I did this or that, I felt him frowning down upon me from wherever he was.

"I know what you mean," I told Lauren, "and of course you're not perfect. I'm not either. No one on this earth is, Lauren, although some of us are kinder than others and use our goodness more fully. All humans make some mistakes—or feel they do because others have different standards—and occasionally have some bad thoughts.

"But don't you ever forget. Lauren Katherine Brenner," I added emphatically, shaking a forefinger for emphasis, "that there's a whole lot of good in you—just oodles and oodles of it—and if Jason can see you, he sees your goodness."

She thought about this for a while and seemed to digest it slowly before she said, "I just don't understand why a little baby like Jason had to die."

Had to die. Lauren had said the phrase almost as if her little brother's death had been preordained, but I didn't really believe in such a thing. Sudden infant death syndrome had felled baby Jason for whatever reason it happens to some babies and not others. I instinctively knew that rather than looking for information about crib death, Lauren searched for some understanding of the great scheme of things. She was coming face-to-face with the universal questions about life and death that haunt us all at some point or another and which have infinite answers and yet, when it comes right down to it, none at all. How timeless is humankind's search for meaning to life and death.

And why indeed does a little child *have to die?* I didn't know. Since I also didn't know Lauren's family's religious affiliation, I thought it best not to supply what might be conflicting views.

"I don't know why he died, Lauren," I told her,

"but have you ever stopped to think that it was not very long ago that nowhere in this great big universe was there any baby Jason? How thrilling that the love your mother and father have for each other could bring him out of nowhere, into being. Some people never have a little Jason at all."

Lauren's eyes deepened to sapphire and grew wide at the thought. "Maybe you can't know where Jason is now, or even if he still is," I continued, "but you can be sure that for having known that little fellow, your life is that much richer."

She was nodding vigorously as a single fat tear slid slowly down her cheek. As I gave her a hug, she said, "He is alive in my heart."

"I know, sweetheart, and that's a very important way for someone to be alive."

The little girl nodded again and blinked back her tears. Wanting her to focus even more upon her little brother's life and upon the tragedy of loss, I asked, "What are your favorite memories of Jason?"

The question seemed to please Lauren, for she quickly dried her brimming eyes and became more animated as the soberness began to dissipate.

"I remember the day we had our picture taken—all four of us—and Mom dressed Jason for the first time in his *big boy* suit. That's what we called it. It was a red jumpsuit and had a little jacket that matched with patches on the elbows, just like Daddy's wool jacket with the patches. Only Jason's was in some soft baby material."

Her smile was nostalgic as she pictured the little boy, and her fresh-washed eyes sparkled.

"And I played a little game with Jason. It was my most favorite thing. Do you want to hear what it was?"

"I certainly do."

"I'd take my finger and make it buzz like a bee and

land it on his tummy. Jason always smiled at me, Lissa, and sometimes he even laughed out loud."

"Those are certainly fine memories, Lauren. What else?" Waiting as I was for her to add something further about the baby, the question she tossed at me took me off guard.

"What's your favorite memory of Jeffrey?"

She had me there, for it was a loaded question if there ever was one. Had I been asked that same question months ago, I could have rattled off any of a dozen wonderful memories with ease, but now what would it be? So much of what I'd held dear had been colored by the discoveries I'd made since Jeffrey's death.

Were the quiet times when we had worked on separate projects in our condo as companionable as they'd seemed, or was Jeffrey working a vasectomy into his busy schedule while I read fifth grade book reports and melted just to see his handsome profile as I walked into the kitchen for more tea?

Was the expensive candy or best champagne he'd occasionally brought home for no special occasion a spontaneous gesture of love, or was it to celebrate the most recent large sum of money deposited into his secret account?

The disturbing thoughts might have continued had not Lauren drawn me back to the present.

"Lissa?"

"His cinnamon rolls," I told the little girl decisively, naming the first thing that popped into my mind that wasn't suspect.

"His cinnamon rolls?"

"Yes. It wasn't just that they tasted scrumptious, which they did. It was fun to wake up some Sunday mornings, smell them baking, and be surprised with rolls he'd made from scratch. He liked to put a fresh flower in a vase on the tray with the rolls and serve me breakfast in bed or at the little table by the bay window. 'Breakfast is served, Princess Petunia,' he would say."

I didn't add that usually we made love after eating the rolls. "That sounds very nice. Jeffrey was nice to do that."

"Yes, he was."

And it had been the little things like that that had, I realized, kept me going, kept me from seeing the overall picture while he was still alive and not liking what it added up to.

When Lauren didn't say anything more, I decided it was time to head back down to the dock for our boat trip back to the island. We were meeting Katherine and Ed for dinner later, and I wanted a little time to shower and change and read the _Baedecker's_ entry on Philae. When I reminded Lauren of the dinner plans, she seemed ready to leave.

As we walked along the Nile after disposing of our pop bottles, Lauren asked out of nowhere, "Why has that man been following us?"

"What man?" I asked as my heart rate kicked into a higher gear. Why on earth would anyone follow us here? Could it be Brown Suit? Maybe I really had seen him at Aswan Airport.

"Oh, I don't know. Just a man," she told me, seeming more curious than worried.

She was being maddeningly vague, and since I really needed an answer, I would have to pry a little.

"Can you point him out to me?"

She did a quick 360-degree scan and told me, "I don't see him now."

What a terrible pair of spies we would make, I thought—you so obvious and I so unaware.

"What does he look like, Lauren?" I asked. I was about to describe the man in the brown suit and then thought better of leading her.

But the man Lauren described was not Brown Suit.

With fingers that had turned as clumsy as sticks of woods, I reached into my purse for the camel snapshot, dropped it, and said as I finally handed it to Lauren, "That sounds like someone I know. Does the man you saw look anything like the man in this picture?"

She looked at the photo carefully.

"That's him," she said, pointing to the only non-Egyptian male. "He's been following us."

CHAPTER FIFTEEN

Even after a session of scenery therapy from my balcony, the idea of the Jeffrey look-alike following Lauren and me through the bazaar—and heaven only knew where else— unnerved me to the extent that, pleading a migraine, I did not meet the Brenners that evening for dinner after all.

Under any circumstance, the sensation of being followed by a stranger must make one's skin crawl. That this one was a dead-ringer for Jeffrey heightened that feeling many times over. I was so taken aback by Lauren's unhesitant identification of the man in the camel photo as the same person she had seen shadowing us that I had, in fact, heard her chatter only as a background buzz as we crossed the water on our way back to Elephantine Island.

As the launch hummed beneath my feet, I asked myself if it could have been the same man in both Upper and Lower Egypt. It could, but it didn't seem likely, at least not as coincidence, when I calculated that Aswan was some 600 miles from Giza.

And yet was Lauren's Jeffrey look-alike my Jeffrey look-alike, or had we chanced to see two separate beings who closely resembled my late husband? There was, I had to admit, a certain universality to his type of tall, dark, handsome good looks, and that that might be the case was probably the only thing that kept my uneasiness from spiraling into panic. Still, I had the first faint stirrings of a headache.

"Are you okay, Lissa?" the little girl asked, jolting me back to the present.

"To tell you the truth," I told her, "I've felt better. It's just a headache, but I think I'll rest in my room for a while after we get back."

"Maybe it was a bad cola," she theorized as we docked.

"Maybe so," I said as I smiled at her concern.

A bad cola . . . or a bad situation.

In my room, once again I stared at the enigmatic figure in the background of the picture I had originally intended to mail to my niece.

"Who are you?" I asked of the man who was and yet was not Jeffrey. Why, his very stance had an identical air of proud self-assurance that might have belonged to a model standing just so, in clothes perfect for the occasion. The safari jacket and hat were exactly what Jeffrey would have selected for a trip to the pyramids.

I remembered how obsessed he could be with his appearance. Looking one's best is one thing, but I saw now that at some point Jeffrey had crossed the line from laudable neatness into narcissism.

One day after jogging together around Green Lake, for instance, I suggested that since we would pass my friend Lori's apartment building on our way home, we drop off the tennis racquet she had left in the trunk of our car. Lori wasn't one for formality and didn't mind drop-ins.

"It will save her a trip to Bellevue," I explained to Jeffrey.

He paused as if to consider the idea and replied, "I don't want her to see me looking like this."

He had on an attractive, almost new jogging outfit, and with his hair just a bit windblown, I thought he look excruciatingly handsome.

"Looking like what? That's one of Nordstrom's best you have on . . ."

"It's ruined," he cut in as he clenched his jaw and took one hand off the steering wheel. "Look," he continued, pointing to what I saw was a very faint yellow smudge, "mustard."

We had had hot dogs after our run, but until the moment he pointed it out to me, I hadn't noticed the tiny splotch of yellow.

"You're so handsome that Lori won't even notice," I told him reassuringly, trying to sympathize with his testy reaction to such a minor detraction. "Lori's always telling me that you look like a million bucks in anything."

Silence.

"Why don't you stay in the car, then, and I'll just run the racquet up to her?"

But no, to my amazement, Jeffrey, apparently afraid that Lori might come out to the car and see the telltale condiment, wouldn't have it that way.

"We're going home," he told me.

And that had been that since he was driving.

Now, when I looked at the man in the picture for the umpteenth time, for a split-second he seemed to be wearing a mustard-stained jogging suit, and I shook my head as I forcefully replaced the troublesome likeness into my purse.

"Enough!" I reprimanded myself as I put it out of sight. Although I was frustrated once again in my effort to reach Steve in Cairo, Katherine was in her room when I called to let her know that the aspirin were helping, and her kindness cheered me considerably. We also sketched out plans for the next day, deciding to have a festive farewell dinner together after going our separate ways during the day.

As we hung up, my stomach growled to remind me that it needed filling, so a bit skeptical that I would get what I wanted, I ordered a good, old-fashioned hamburger on a bun. I'd tried a grilled ham and cheese sandwich in Greece that had been a culinary disaster. To my pleasure, though, the Egyptian hamburger could have passed muster at the finest American gourmet burger restaurant.

I slept better than I had expected to.

The next day was a medley of sightseeing, introspection and the mounting realization that time with Lauren and her grandparents was growing much too short.

Over dinner that night in the hotel's Nashwa Club, which featured belly dancers and a cultural show with Nubian musicians and dancers, we enjoyed the entertainment, our food and talking about our respective experiences during the day.

The Brenners had gone to see the Aswan High Dam, while I had opted for Philae.

Ed especially, had been agog during their trip to the great dam, *el-Sadd el-Ali*, a huge structure of 55.9 billion cubic yards of stones and sand, with a clay core and concrete facing materials making it seventeen times the volume of the Pyramid of Cheops.

"Two and one-fourth miles long it was," he said wonderingly after rattling off the dam's other dimensions.

"We walked right on top of it," Lauren said.

"I was amazed at how quiet it was," Katherine remarked. "There were some of the dogs," Lauren added, "like the ones we saw at Deir el-Bahri."

"I'll bet they were doing the same thing," I commented, remembering how the dogs had sprung to life in the Necropolis of Thebes.

"How big did they say the lake is again, Ed?" Katherine asked her husband in reference to Lake Nasser, the great reservoir of water behind the dam.

"Three hundred and seventeen miles long, I think, Kath,"

Ed replied, seemingly pleased to be turned to for information. Theirs seemed to be such a good marriage that I wasn't sure if Katherine had really forgotten that tidbit or had asked expressly because she knew her husband reveled in being counted on when it came to such matters.

We then launched into a discussion—a debate at some points—of the positive and the negative aspects of the High Dam. On one hand, it had provided irrigation to regions that couldn't count on it before and supplied electricity to the burgeoning population in urban areas along the river.

On the other hand, however, the age-old natural pattern of inundation had been forever altered, so that some regions had lost much of their precious alluvium. "And the crocodiles," as Lauren piped up. Even worse for those directly in the path of *progress*, forty-two Nubian villages had been drowned, according to the Brenners' guide, leaving thousands of people homeless with the building of the dam.

"I feel sorry for them," Lauren said.

"So do I," I agreed, aware that many Egyptians were bitter.

"Our guide said that if the dam ever breaks, it would devastate Egypt, wiping out most of the population,"

Katherine said as she shook her head and put down her fork.

"That's a chilling thought," I said as I pictured a huge wall of water drowning the populated regions of the Nile Valley. Karnak and a host of other priceless monuments would also disappear.

"Barring sabotage on a grand scale, it shouldn't happen," Ed tried to reassure us.

"Tell us about your day, Lissa," Katherine said after shaking her head again, obviously eager to dispel the grim picture that had crossed our minds.

"Was Philae spooky?" Lauren asked.

"Just in a couple of spots. It was wonderful in another way so light and airy. I could have stayed up there all day," I told her as I thought again of the way the cerulean sky and deeper blue water made a perfect foil to the whitish stone temple complex, and how the combination of breeze and sunshine had made the weather just perfect.

The approach by steamer had been dramatic in itself, since the temples had first appeared like a mirage from afar and then ever-closer, from different angles, as we rounded the island and spied the almost dainty little Kiosk of Trajan near the bulky pylons dominating the small piece of land.

"That's the place that was moved block by block from one island to another, wasn't it, to save it from the rising waters when the dam was built?" Ed asked.

I told him it was, and as I thought of the Temple of Isis, as well as the beautiful reliefs of flute players and harpists in the Temple of Hathor, I also told Ed my opinion that having deliberately destroyed Philae would have been a crime.

"I'll second that," he said.

"If I had a lot of money, I would go around saving temples," Lauren put in with conviction that had turned her delicate face resolute.

"Good for you," I told her as her grandparents agreed. "From what I read in the guidebook, it sounds as though there's a lot left to see," Katherine remarked.

"Yes, it's Ptolemaic and not as ancient as some of the other temple complexes we've seen in Egypt," I explained as I mentioned a few of the high points.

"Ptolemaic," Lauren repeated, liking the word. "What's Ptolemaic?"

I told her that the Ptolemies had ruled Egypt centuries after Hatshepsut, who continued to be Lauren's touchstone to a fabled past.

"Cleopatra was a Ptolemy," Ed told his granddaughter.

Just then, a belly dancer in a ruby costume burst through a door at the side of the room, hopped onto the stage and began her undulations to Egyptian music as Lauren poked me in the ribs and whispered that I had better watch carefully as my first lesson in what I would be doing in the outfit we had purchased together.

"I told Grandma and Gramps," she told me, giggling, as I lovingly called her a scamp.

As lively as the show was, the little girl's eyelids soon grew heavy, and by mutual agreement, we left between acts. The Brenner family would leave from Aswan Airport for Cairo early in the morning and then be off for St. Louis the following day, while I would return to Luxor before flying back to Cairo for more time there.

"See you in the morning," the sleepy child told me as her grandfather opened the door with a key suspended from a brass ankh. As they entered the room, Katherine and I, both happy about Lauren's brighter spirits, chatted for a few minutes in the hallway about the little girl, since we weren't sure we'd have much time in the morning.

As we parted, she said, "You'll let me know what

happens with Steve now, won't you, dear?"

As I assured her I would and began walking down the hall to my own room, though, I wondered myself what would happen, and my resolve to find Steve in led to still another fruitless phone call.

After breakfast together in the Orangery buffet early the next morning, Katherine and Ed gave Lauren and me some time to ourselves before their departure for the airport.

As the little girl and I sat side-by-side on a couch in a lobby adorned with a profusion of salmon-colored gladioli, I felt a lump in my throat as I watched Lauren's delicate chin quiver.

"I'm going to miss you, Lissa," she told me as her delphinium-colored eyes puddled up. My own eyes were no less misty.

"Oh, I'm going to miss you, too, sweetheart," I told the child I'd grown to love in such a short time.

"Do you feel better about your husband?"

Struck by her directness, I wasn't sure what to reply. Did I feel better? Yes and no. On the plus side, I had worked out some of the heartbreak of shattered dreams, but the image of the loving husband who had served me homemade rolls in bed still clashed with that of the stranger who had had a vasectomy and a secret bank account—maybe even a lover in Cairo. For what it was worth, I realized now that I had loved an illusion. Although I might never be certain how well the real Jeffrey matched my ideal, I did feel ready to let go and embrace the future. I would survive. The persistent feeling of something left undone would surely dissipate.

"Sometimes yes and sometimes no," I ended up telling Lauren candidly.

"But not quite as 'whopsed up?'" she said with an endearing smile. My grandmother's expression still sounded odd on the child's lips and brought a smile to my face.

"Not quite as whopsed up," I agreed. "How about you?"

"I'm mostly smoothed out."

"That's great news."

"I have something for you," I told her as I reached into my purse.

"You do?"

"Wear it for good luck," I told her as I winked and handed her a small box, which she opened slowly, obviously relishing the mystery of what might be inside.

Then the lid was off and her eyes sparkled like sapphires.

"A scarab! Oh, Lissa, I love it," she said as she lifted the tiny golden beetle from its nest of cotton. "Thank you. It's just like my favorite thing at Karnak."

"I know. That's why it's a scarab instead of something else," I told her as I helped her put the charm onto her neck chain. The beetle was petite and suited her well.

"I have something for you, too. You'll never guess what it is," the little girl sang as she produced a box a little larger than the one I had given her.

I made a show of opening mine as carefully as Lauren had hers.

"Ah! Your favorite thing, Lauren. A scarab! This is beautiful," I told her as I lifted the beetle from its box and admired it. "Thank you so much."

Exquisitely crafted in gold with bright lapis-lazuli forming its wings, it was like the ones I had seen in Luxor. I knew it was a fine piece of jewelry and was deeply touched.

"I will wear it often," I told Lauren.

"Me too. Now we each have one," she remarked as she clapped her hands together in pleasure.

I removed the filigree heart charm adorning my chain and slid on the scarab before refastening it around my neck.

"Perfect," Lauren proclaimed. "It matches your eyes." We exchanged addresses and phone numbers but had talked only a little more before Katherine and Ed appeared on the staircase. A boy had brought their luggage down on the elevator, which naturally Katherine was avoiding at all costs.

"It's time," Ed said as they neared us.

We showed off our respective scarabs, promised to visit in St. Louis or Portland if we could, and then with hugs and damp eyes, we said our goodbyes.

My plane didn't leave for Luxor until hours later, so I decided to visit Kom Ombo, one of Aunt Miriam's *seconds* on the must-see list, about twenty-five miles from Aswan. Had time permitted, I would have gone as far as Edfu, but that would have to wait for another trip.

Although nothing could have induced me to drive in Cairo, the roads looked a bit tamer in Upper Egypt they at least had far less traffic—so I ended up renting a small car when I couldn't find a tour that would take me there and get me back to Aswan in plenty of time to catch my plane.

A strange thing, the cult of the crocodile had fascinated Aunt Miriam, and Kom Ombo, I knew, had once been a center of crocodile worship. As I dodged donkeys here and there and passed more biblical-seeming farming scenes, I tried to imagine the fear the people along the Nile must have had of the large reptile when great numbers of them, exacting heavy tolls upon the lives of animals and people alike, had still basked along the sunny riverbanks and on small islands of sand.

I had never actually seen a crocodile, but I remembered a time when I was in Florida, in a park on an island where one could drive through and note the varied wildlife that included alligators floating like logs in the water. Although numerous signs had been posted to the effect that only an idiot would provoke an alligator, some people have to learn the hard way. In an isolated area by an expanse of still water where several of them drifted like huge pieces of bark, a man had approached us and asked where all the 'gators were. When Dad told him that the *logs* were alligators, the man had scoffed and thrown a stick at one of them to prove he was right. At that, the *log*" had come to life as if a current had been switched on, and I'd never forgotten its speed or the man's hasty retreat.

From everything I had heard, crocodiles were even more fearsome. Perhaps in the hope that the great reptiles would not attack the faithful, since fear has a way of giving rise to means of appeasement, those living along some parts of the Nile had worshipped crocodiles.

Rom Ombo turned out to be quite off the beaten path, way out in the country, but it immediately caught my fancy. Overlooking a bend in the river, the temple was up high, and the commanding view, fresh air and mute reminders of crocodile worship, including their mummies on display, were unique.

Maybe when I spotted several ancient stone sarcophagi, empty but seeming to lie in wait, still, for occupants, I should have taken them as an omen, but I didn't.

Instead, I spent the next hour or so wandering amid colonnades, a hypostyle hall that was tiny in comparison to Karnak's but which featured columns with many kinds of capitals, and great reliefs showing sacrifices to the gods made by the Ptolemies. The perfectly paired Sanctuaries of Sobek, who appeared in human form but with a crocodile's head, and the falcon-headed Haroeris (Horus the Elder) stood side-by-side as if a pen had indelibly bisected the area longitudinally to give each god his due.

Outside the temple, I noted the Nilometer, a deep well with a spiral staircase inside, which, important to farming and taxation purposes, had once gauged the rise and fall of the Nile. When I peered over the rim, I was surprised at its depth. Black water stood motionless far below me, and I could see the circular stone steps snaking around. A little to my surprise, two tourists had found their way into the fascinating measuring device and stood on the stairs.

Although I had no intention of descending those steps to stand on the stone landing above the dark, still water, I did want to get an idea of how people had accessed the Nilometer in its working days.

A bit of detective work led me around the perimeter of the well, to the discovery of some stone stairs that apparently led down to the spiral staircase and the landing not far above water level. I doubted very much that the people were supposed to be within the Nilometer, for a metal waist high bar blocked my way. From where I was, I couldn't actually see into the well.

"Tourists," I muttered under my breath as I stepped under the bar just far enough to see if they were still inside. They were nowhere in sight, and the place suddenly seemed forbidding. I'd found the way into the Nilometer, however, and was satisfied.

As I emerged from beneath the bar to the safety of the other stairs, I heard a grunt followed by thumping sound. To my astonishment, from seemingly out of nowhere, a man crumpled at my feet on the stairs leading up and out.

A coronary? Had he tripped? Then to my disbelief, I saw a blossom of red seeping through the fabric of his baggy brown suit.

Brown Suit!

Instinct told me to flee the scene as quickly as possible, that I might be in danger myself, but I couldn't leave a man bleeding near the entrance to a water-filled shaft. Leaning close to him, I saw the rise and fall of his chest and knew he was, at least, alive.

I ran up to the stop of the stairway and looked around. Where were all the tourists when I needed one? No one was in sight.

I raced back down to look at Brown Suit again. The spot of blood was not large, but it was on his left side, how near his heart I wasn't certain.

At that moment, his eyes fluttered open. "Are you all right?" I asked.

"Go, Miss McKinnon," he told me softly but clearly in that precise English accent many Egyptians have. "You are in danger here."

"I can't just leave you here." He began coughing.

"You must. Tell a bus driver there is someone hurt in the well. Then," he paused to cough, "go. Do not come back. Stay away from the American professor with blond hair." More coughing followed.

"All right. Don't talk more. I'll get someone to you as fast as I can."

As I sped from the well, past the sarcophagi, and on down from the temple site, I thought I heard his soft murmur of thanks.

CHAPTER SIXTEEN

I felt almost limp from confusion and disbelief in the wake of the alarming turn of events at Kom Ombo. How I longed to talk to Steve! Of course there was no telephone in this remote remnant of the cult of the crocodile, and I had no assurance, even if there had been, that his phone wouldn't just have rung forlornly again anyway. Shakily, I drove back to Aswan.

If I hadn't already had an Egyptian Air ticket to Luxor, I think I might have bypassed that town completely and headed straight back to Cairo. But Luxor it was since nothing left for Cairo until much later than my shuttle to Luxor. I wanted to leave Aswan as quickly as possible. Since I had left Bastet I at the Luxor jeweler's and was reluctant to entrust it to the vagaries of the mail system, perhaps it was for the best.

Feeling safer in the air, I was tempted to let myself downplay the strange drama at Kom Ombo, but unfortunately I remembered only too well the horrible anemone of blood blossoming through the worn fabric of the brown gabardine suit and couldn't allow myself that luxury.

Brown Suit had definitely been hurt.

Even though he had implored me verbally and with a matching plea in his dark eyes to leave him where he lay and see to my own safety, and although I had found a bus driver to summon medical help for him, I still felt negligent for having left the temple site without knowing how the injured man was.

Or who he was. That he had wanted me out of danger seemed evident, but ally or not, why had he shadowed me in the first place? And what, exactly, was the danger? Whatever the case, I could no longer believe that running into him at far-flung spots throughout Egypt had been coincidental, for he had known my name.

Stay away from the American professor with blond hair, rang Brown Suit's words through my brain like the reverberations of a gong.

American. Professor.

Blond.

"Where are you, Steve?" my mind hummed to the whine of the jet engines. Not for a moment did I take the mysterious Egyptian's warning to heart, but I needed contact with the man who fit Brown Suit's description to a T. I just wanted to hear his voice. I could try to decipher Brown Suit's meaning later and maybe even learn how, and who he was.

All things considered, I thought I would feel safer in Cairo.

Toward that end, once on the ground in Luxor, I tried to get an evening flight back to the city but had no luck. I would have to stay the night in Luxor.

My hotel looked as it had a few days earlier, right down to the same little scarlet-uniformed boy at the door, but it wasn't the same for me. Not only was I disturbed by what had transpired, but this time I'd hear no nine-year-old voice call my name, nor would I see the spun-gold hair flying as Lauren cannonballed into the pool. Had it really been only that morning that we'd kissed goodbye?

The first thing I did after checking in and getting settled into a room was to call Steve, who for the fifth or sixth time in the past few days did not answer. Where was he? Could something have happened to him? I replaced the receiver in an irritation born out of anxiety, thinking that if I didn't reach him soon, I would have to call his aunt or someone else who might know his whereabouts.

I might have revisited Karnak or one of the area's many other popular attractions, but I no longer felt safe out on my own at this point, especially as evening approached, and I wasn't really in the mood for sightseeing anyway.

I retrieved the troublesome Bastet and the custom-made cartouches from the jewelry shop after a dinner I didn't really taste. The personalized gifts had turned out beautifully, and fortunately no one would ever guess by looking that the slender stone cat had ever been broken.

From my room, I watched the persimmon sun drop behind the bulk of the famous tomb area across the Nile and remembered my excursion there with Lauren. I would always treasure my day in the necropolis with her, but I had hoped to return there, and to Karnak, with Steve. I still didn't know why he had cancelled out on our Luxor plans after we had made them so enthusiastically.

Was he, as Katherine Brenner had suggested, reluctant to see me and afraid of his feelings and how the brief romantic interlude might affect our friendship?

Did he know something new about Jeffrey, perhaps having found out where Jeffrey was buried?

Or had Steve merely had an inspired period of creativity he couldn't ignore?

When I decided to try reaching him still again, this time, a little to my surprise, he answered his phone, and I jumped to hear his voice on the heels of all my failed attempts.

"Hi, Steve," I said, "it's Lissa."

Instead of a regular greeting, I heard a voice suffused with anger ask, "Where in blazes have you been, Lissa?"

Where had I been? For all the response I had from him, he could have been in a Turkish back alley, throat slit. It's strange how certain worry-inspired scenarios seem ridiculous only after we know a loved one is safe.

"I might ask you the same," I said, trying to keep my voice steady. "Didn't you get my message telling you I'd gone south?"

"Yes, but how cryptic can you get? 'Gone to Abu Simbel. Back in three days.' No hotel. No phone number. No way of reaching you."

He was really ticked off.

"1 didn't mean to worry you," I told him with feeling, realizing that perhaps he had had similar back alley visions of me. "I went there via Aswan with the Brennerls."

"The Brenners?"

"The American girl Lauren and her grandparents," I reminded him. "We had a very good time."

"I'm glad to hear it."

"Now it's your turn. Where have you been, Steve? I tried calling you several times over the past few days. I was getting a little worried, especially after the way you so abruptly changed our plans."

There was a pause.

"Steve?"

"I'm sorry if I worried you, Lissa, and I appreciate your concern.

I've just been in and out a lot, sketching," he told me, and something—a certain flatness in his voice—made me wonder if he was telling the whole truth, which was an unusual thought, considering that Steve had always, as far as I knew, told me the truth.

Let it ride, I thought, as I decided to give him some room and not analyze this call too minutely. At least I knew he was all right.

Explanations could come in person; "Good," I returned. "You will have to show me the fruits of your labors when I get back to Cairo."

"That I will," he said, sounding more normal, "and I'll want a blow-by-blow account of your adventures in Nubia."

"I won't spare you a detail," I promised, wondering how he would take it if I mentioned having been followed through a bazaar by a man who looked like Jeffrey and then having found Brown Suit bleeding near the entrance to the Nilometer at Kom Ombo. "Adventures" was the word, all right.

In a softer voice, he asked, "Are you all right, Lissa? Your voice sounds—I don't know—overly bright."

"I'm fine."

I was tempted to ask if he had heard anything new from Turkey, but since I trusted Steve to let me know straight out if he'd discovered anything worth telling about Jeffrey's final days and death, I didn't.

As for Brown Suit, now that I had Steve on the other end of the line, I realized that to tell him over the phone, when I was so many miles away, would only worry him.

And oh yes, my heart murmured, *I'm in love with you.* So much left unsaid!

"And you, Steve? Are you all right?" I finally asked.

"Of course," he assured me, "just a bit tired. I'm sure

I'll be bright-eyed and bushy-tailed by the time you see me, and we can talk then."

"About that, I've decided to fly back to Cairo tomorrow."

"You're angry because I postponed meeting you in Luxor. I'm really sorry, Lissa."

"No . . . no, I'm not angry."

I think I expected him to try to coax me into staying in Luxor until he could meet me, but he didn't do that, surprising me a little.

"Well, maybe it's for the best that you're returning. Let me have the flight information and I'll be at the airport."

As we rang off after I gave him the information, I thought it had been a rather unsatisfactory call. We hadn't said much. Yet at least we had finally made contact with each other, and we could do some better talking tomorrow.

I didn't know how things would deteriorate in person.

First of all, the cat was literally out of the bag—sort of—upon my arrival in Cairo.

After giving each other chaste pecks on the cheek at the airport, Steve had taken hold of my tote bag and remarked with a certain twinkle males often get in their eyes when lifting women's heavy purses, "What did you do? Bring back part of Karnak?"

"I'll take that," I said rather abruptly, grabbing the bag away with more force than I had intended. The moment I had, I wished I could take back the gesture. It was just that I didn't want Steve to find the Bastet at this point and spoil Aunt Miriam's surprise after I'd carried it around, broken it and had it repaired.

The twinkle was gone, and I had to say something.

"That was rude of me, Steve. I'm sorry." I should have left it at that but, uncustomaryly fibbing to Steve, I added, "The weight of the bag is from a soapstone statuette I bought near Karnak for a teacher friend, and I've gotten used to protecting my bag, especially after having one snatched in Upper Egypt."

Steve seemed mollified.

"I've always liked the soapstone figures, especially the Bastets," he commented, and it was difficult not to chuckle since little did he know that this was not only a Bastet but a Bastet earmarked for him, even if it didn't appear to be soapstone.

Dressed in jeans and a polo shirt, he looked tired, I thought, and every bit as preoccupied as Lauren had been a few days earlier.

Conversation fell rather flat in the car on the way to the Nile Hilton, where I would be staying this time. Remembering the hotel's proximity to the museum and downtown Cairo, I'd changed my mind at the last minute and was lucky enough to find a room. Although I was eager enough to tell Steve about my positive experiences in Upper Egypt, I didn't want to sock him with the negative ones while he was maneuvering through heavy traffic. To avoid blurting out what I wasn't ready to say, I said little, and for whatever reason he had, so did he.

I thought I'd found a "safe" topic.

"How's the sketching going?" I asked. Unexpectedly, the question seemed to irritate him.

"Fine, just fine," he told me without much inflection.

"You don't sound very enthusiastic."

"I guess I've hit a creative slump or something," he told me, trying to smile and just barely making it.

He oozed tension. His knuckles were white as they gripped the steering wheel. Did I make him feel that uneasy? When I remembered the closeness of our last ride into Cairo, from Saqqara, the contrast nearly broke my heart.

"Your muse will come back," I told him. "The doors I saw in your folio last week were exquisitely done."

"I'm glad you think so," he remarked, not unkindly, but he seemed so uncommunicative that I let the conversation lapse.

That's when I identified the familiar aroma that wafted my way from inside the car and which had been teasing me. It made me think of my grandfather cherry wood pipe tobacco.

It also made me think back to smelling cherry wood tobacco in my Luxor hotel room after the day in the necropolis with Lauren, and I wondered again if an intruder had been inside.

"Is something wrong?" Steve asked,

When I mentioned the familiar scent, he told me an acquaintance had been in his car earlier that day.

"It makes me think of my grandfather," I told him, not saying anything about Luxor.

A smile was there, but strained, and I yearned for our old easiness together. Would it ever be the same? Had we ruined our friendship after all?

Now that I knew I was in love with him, the thought that perhaps he didn't share my new awareness was devastating. What if he felt disgusted by what had passed between us? I didn't know if I could maintain a friendship in that case, since I couldn't turn back my emotional clock and undo my longing to feel his arms around me.

But if Katherine had been right in her assessment of the situation, Steve was sitting there, tense, because he, too, felt what I did and was reluctant to chance making the wrong move. Had not his hands been frozen around the steering wheel, I think that, heavy traffic or none, I would have taken one of his in mine, just to let him know I still cared and wasn't sorry about what had happened, and to gauge how he felt.

Instead, we made desultory small talk about Cairo's usual hustle and bustle as we made our way to the hotel, where he pulled the car into the entranceway, parked it temporarily, and walked into the lobby with me.

"I'll stay with your bags while you check in," he told me as he took a seat near the windows.

I had to wait in line at the busy desk. When it was finally my turn to register, if the desk clerk hadn't happened to have been called into a back room for a moment, I probably never would have seen what I did.

With the lull in the registration process, I turned around and glanced at Steve, who, unaware of my eyes upon him, had unwrapped the Bastet and was holding it. In astonishment, I watched him examine the little statue as if trying to decipher its hieroglyphic good luck inscription. Then, just as the desk clerk returned, I saw Steve's forefinger trace the seam where the parts were fastened together.

By the time I had my room key and had walked back to him, the rewrapped Bastet was back inside my tote bag as if nothing had happened. For some reason, I said nothing about what I'd seen.

I was deflated when he left right after that, letting a bellboy help me to my room with my luggage, but I felt a trifle better again when he suggested that we have dinner later in the Hilton's best restaurant.

The word *lovely* has a good number of applications. The atmosphere of the restaurant was romantically so, the veal was succulent, and our wine was just right. Steve looked handsome in a navy blazer, and I was wearing a favorite off-white dress trimmed with gold buttons.

But *lovely's* meaning didn't extend to cover what was happening between Steve and me. We just didn't seem to click, and it obviously made him as uneasy as it did me.

Although he tried not to show it, he wasn't even especially enthusiastic about Karnak and Abu Simbel when I talked about them—certainly not the Steve I knew. It was as if what I said captured his interest and yet something like a throbbing tooth distracted him and ruined his pleasure. For this reason, I still hadn't said anything about the down side of my Nubian trip.

We were nearing the end of our meal when I finally said, "Would you like to tell me what's bothering you, Steve?"

He gave me a tentative smile and said, "I will soon, Lissa. I'm sorry if I'm not good company. Maybe I'm coming down with something."

"I hope not. Would you like to call it a night?"

"Thanks, but no, I'm not that uncomfortable."

But something was wrong. I saw it in the way his eyes only skimmed over mine, and I heard it in his voice. I took a sip of Beaujolais, and as I set my glass back down and looked at Steve, he was watching me intently for the first time of the evening.

"What's wrong?" I asked again.

He ran his fingers through his luxuriant hair. "Lissa,

what would you do if Jeffrey were alive?"

He might as well have prodded me with a hot poker. "Alive! Good heavens, what did you find out, Steve?"

"Whoa! I didn't mean to alarm you. It was only a theoretical question."

I could tell that he regretted his approach to the topic, as I did my reaction. Since we had had the habit of asking each other theoretical questions, I should have known where he was coming from. As usual, however, Jeffrey's name had a way of being a spark to the dry tinder of our emotions. Or mine at least.

I relaxed a bit and considered Steve's question.

How would I feel? Stunned. I'd feel totally stunned. The very idea of mourning a living man—of going through such agony for nothing—made my blood run cold. And oh, if it happened to me, I would shake my fist at fate, at whatever you want to call it, for having let me grieve, longing for Jeffrey and then finally letting go as I accepted his death, only to find out he was alive after I had fallen in love with another man. But it was an emotional color that suffused my mind, and I felt as incapable of articulating it as a person does the color chartreuse to a blind person who has never experienced the spectrum.

"It's something I can't really put into words, Steve. I'd be shocked to my toes. I would laugh and cry and heaven only knows what else, I'm sure."

"And joy? Would you feel joy?"

"Of course," I told him, for even with the complex and painful repercussions of a live Jeffrey, his life itself would be cause for celebration.

"That's what I thought," Steve replied dispiritedly.

Spark to the tinder or none, I had to ask, "What did you find out?"

"It's been a will-o'-the-wisp type of pursuit. I'm still following up on a lead. So far, though, I haven't found Jeffrey's grave."

"You'll let me know if you do?"

"Of course I will. I'll even take you there if you want to go." It didn't seem the time to mention the Jeffrey look-alike Lauren had seen in Aswan. Theoretical was one thing; flesh and blood, another.

After tea for me and coffee for Steve, we took the elevator down to my floor and he walked me to my room. When I fumbled with the key in the lock, he took it from my hand and opened the door. He didn't step inside, and I didn't invite him, since I'd resolved not to have him in my room again until I knew how he felt about us. Now, though, on the threshold, I felt myself melting and had to fight the temptation to throw my resolve out the window. More than anything else, I wanted him to hold me and tell me everything was all right.

When our eyes met as he handed the key back to me, he must have seen the naked desire in my eyes. For a moment, I thought I saw a matching longing in his, and I reached my hand up and out to caress his cheek. He groaned and pulled me to him.

My heart hardly had the chance to sing, however, before he had thrust me away.

"We can't do this, Lissa."

"Tell me why. I . . ."

"No," he said, putting a hand over my mouth, "don't say it.

I can't explain. Not yet."

He was turning to leave.

"Wait! You can't just leave."

"I have to," he told me as he began walking.

"I'll see you for lunch tomorrow."

Puzzled and hurt, I let him go.

As I stepped into my room, I saw a rectangle of beige paper at my feet. An envelope without a postmark, it had my name on it and bore the ram's head logo of the hotel in Luxor.

Strange, I thought as I picked it up. Who would write to me from there?

When I broke the seal, within the envelope I found a sheet of thin notepaper and a smaller, plain envelope.

The note read: "Sorry. My employee forgot to give you the enclosed paper. It was inside your cat." The note was signed with a name that didn't ring a bell.

My cat? The jeweler, I realized, still puzzled. I hadn't the slightest idea what else might have been inside Bastet I hadn't a key been enough—and a strange reluctance to find out washed over me.

The envelope was not sealed. When I lifted its flap, I extracted a single, much-folded square of onionskin paper. Carefully, so as not to tear the fragile paper, I slowly uncreased the square.

With a start, I immediately recognized it as a door.

Red, it featured elaborate, large-winged angels that looked like heavenly sentinels.

CHAPTER SEVENTEEN

C uriouser and curiouser, I thought as I awakened the following morning after a restless night fraught with hurt and bewilderment over Steve's strangeness. The slip of paper from the jeweler was also a mystery, and I wondered how I had missed it when the key had fallen out of the statuette.

I looked at the piece of onionskin again in broad daylight, for some reason wanting it not to be the same red door I had seen depicted so beautifully in Steve's folio, but although this was a less finished piece of art, it was unmistakably the same portal Steve had found in Cairo's City of the Dead as a candidate for his book-in-progress.

A key and a picture of a door hidden within the same receptacle strongly suggested that the key was to that door, but why on earth would Aunt Miriam have troubled herself to create such a bizarre route to Steve's gift, and why would anyone hide a surprise in a necropolis?

As I showered and dressed, the questions buzzed like troublesome hornets in my brain. I did have to admit that Aunt Miriam was on the eccentric side. For one thing, she always named her cars—*Whitey Ford* was white and so named because it was not a Ford—and talked to her plants, which she named after fictional characters, and now that I thought of it, one time she had set up a treasure hunt for Steve's birthday. Did this have her stamp on it after all?

When I looked at my watch and calculated that it wouldn't be an ungodly hour in Seattle, I decided to phone Steve's aunt and play it by ear. If she happened to be having a good day—for she had marked ups and downs with her chemo—I would broach the topic of the Bastet. If not, I would let it go and keep my call brief. Whatever the case, I knew she would welcome a call from Cairo, and I was more than ready to comment upon a few of the must-sees she had recommended.

"Lissa!" she exclaimed in a strong voice when she heard me greet her and ask how she was. "You're calling all the way from Cairo? What a delightful surprise. How do you like Egypt so far, dear?"

"I love it, Aunt Miriam. It's certainly everything you said it would be," I told her enthusiastically, which launched discussion about various sites and scenes. I could tell by her voice that she savored the fresh details about the land she loved.

"I hope I can get back there," she commented wistfully.

"So do I, Aunt Miriam," I told her with feeling. "How are you doing?"

"To tell you the truth, this chemo is the pits, Lissa, much worse than the surgery. It knocks me out, and then just as I finally feel more like my old self and ready to do things, as I am now, they zap me with another round of poison. But my doctor thinks it's working, and that makes it worth it."

"It certainly does."

She switched the topic away from herself by asking,

"How's that nephew of mine?"

How I wished I knew. I wondered what she would say if I told her my fear that Steve and I had ruined our friendship. Even though I had a strong hunch that Aunt Miriam would understand, and maybe even applaud, the romantic direction our relationship had taken, any romance seemed definitely on hold, and I steered clear of the subject by telling her that he was fine and made the perfect tour guide.

After we'd talked a bit about his artwork, it seemed time to mention the Bastet. "Aunt Miriam, to change the subject, I have some bad news and some good news."

"The bad first, dear, always the bad first."

"I dropped the Bastet," I blurted, still ashamed of my carelessness on the train.

"You dropped the Bastet?"

"The base and the body separated, but it's been repaired and looks as good as new. I didn't reinsert the key, but that's safely inside my make-up kit."

"Child, I don't understand a word of what you're telling me." Thinking that her end of the call perhaps had some static, I raised my voice slightly and asked, "Can you hear me better now? You are coming through fine."

"I hear you perfectly, Lissa, but what's this about a Bastet and a key?"

I felt a prickle of foreboding as I heard the puzzlement in her voice, for although it had crossed my mind that she might not know about the key or the paper inside the Bastet, I hadn't considered that Aunt Miriam might also know nothing about the stone cat itself.

"What do you mean?" I asked her, deciding that I must have read something into her voice. "The Bastet you arranged for me to bring home as your gift to Steve."

"A Bastet for Steve?" she asked, and this time I couldn't deny the tone of her voice. "But I never made such a request. Tell me why you thought I did."

What in the world? How did I come to have the statuette if not from her?

I explained how it had been delivered to me at the Mena House, along with a note saying that since it was to be a surprise for Steve from her, I was to keep mum about it.

"And you say it's a Bastet? What does it look like?"

I described the blue stone cat.

"You didn't have to pay anyone anything, did you?" she asked.

"No."

"And you say a key was inside the cat? How odd."

"Yes, a space had been hollowed out inside its body."

"What does it look like?"

"The key? It's an old-fashioned type shaped to fit what I think of as a classic keyhole, like the one in the door in *Alice in Wonderland*."

"Yes," she replied, "I know the kind you mean. Why a key purportedly from me was in a Bastet, though, I have absolutely no idea. Do you have any idea what it might unlock?"

"I was coming to that. This may sound bizarre, but I think it's to a tomb or mourner's room in the necropolis here in Cairo. You see," I explained, "there was also a tiny slip of paper within the cat, and I recognized the drawing on it as one of the portals Steve sketched in the necropolis. I remembered the door because it was of elaborate bas-relief, in a shade of red that reminded me of carnelians."

"I don't like the way this sounds. Lissa, you may have gotten yourself mixed up in some kind of intrigue. Please be careful." She paused momentarily, as if thinking, and then said, "Does Steve know about this?"

"No. I haven't said a word to him since I thought the cat was going to be a surprise to him from you." I didn't mention that I had seen Steve surreptitiously inspecting the Bastet in the lobby while I registered.

"Maybe it's time you share this with him. But I don't have to tell you to, do I? You two have always been like a couple of peas in a pod."

Two peas in a pod. Would we ever feel that way again?

Thinking of yesterday's stilted conversation and the way he left me so abruptly last night, I wondered.

"Yes, we were." The past tense had popped out of my mouth unbidden, much to my consternation. I hoped Aunt Miriam wouldn't pick up on it, but I had no such luck.

"Were?" she asked.

"I meant *are*," I tried to correct, but she was too sharp to have missed it.

"What's wrong, Lissa?" she asked in a no-nonsense voice shot through with caring.

"I don't know if you'd call it wrong. It's nothing to worry about. We can talk about it after I get back to the States."

But she wouldn't have it that way.

"I'm listening now, dear."

What had I gotten myself into? The last thing I wanted was to worry a woman thousands of miles away who was undergoing chemo, but not saying anything now would worry her more, if I knew Aunt Miriam.

"It's hard to explain," I told her as I grasped for words.

"You know how Steve and I have always been buddies? I don't know what got into us—maybe the spell of this ancient land—but when we watched the sun set behind the Pyramids of Giza a few days ago, something suddenly seemed different."

"Something ignited?"

"Ignited," I repeated, thinking what a perfect word it was for what had happened that evening, even if the "ignition" had been doused. "Yes, and ever since, we've been so unnatural with each other and, I don't know, miserable."

My eyes suddenly felt as if they were the High Dam holding back the Nile.

Aunt Miriam must have heard the misery in my voice, because she said, "I wish I could give you a hug. Lissa dear, it will work out. Change, even when it's for the better, can take some getting used to," she counseled. Then, "How do you feel about what happened?"

"I don't want our friendship to be ruined."

"I doubt that it will be. It sounds as though your friendship has sprouted wings and that both of you are just still afraid to fly."

Before I could comment, she added, "I'm feeling tired now, so I had better say adieu soon. Your call has made my day. You be careful, Lissa. Tell Steve about the Bastet, and you just remember that a friendship with a solid base endures change. It prevails."

"I'll do that. You take care now."

"I will. Give Steve my love and keep some for yourself."

"Love to you, too, Aunt Miriam. Es-salamu 'alekum!" I wished her, using the Arabic for "Peace be upon you."

"We-'alekum es-salam!" Aunt Miriam replied as we hung up.

"And peace and God's mercy be upon you."

In a strange way that didn't make all that much sense, our conversation had given me a little more to go on than I'd had before. I didn't have the foggiest idea why the Bastet had been directed to me, or by whom, but at least I did know now that I hadn't been carrying around a surprise for Steve. And to think I'd lugged that heavy little beast from Memphis all the way up the Nile to Luxor!

As I thought of Luxor, Karnak came to mind, and I realized that the theft of my tote bag there probably had not been random. Had someone watched me examine Bastet II, thinking it was Bastet I, and grabbed it?

More importantly, was whoever had snatched it still following me?

Aunt Miriam had used the word *intrigue*, and it did seem that I was in the midst of something of that kind. I was a character in a drama whose script I did not have. What my role was, except as some kind of *carrier of the cat*, though, I had no idea. And was Brown Suit another player?

The nature of whatever lay behind the red door had, with Aunt Miriam's denial, suddenly changed from a loving surprise to, quite possibly, something of great value, to have inspired such nefariousness. Although I was curious, I did know that wild horses couldn't drag me to the City of the Dead to look behind the door.

Since the Bastet was not a gift for Steve, I was free to tell him everything connected with the statuette at lunchtime. The more I considered both the key and the strange piece of onionskin having been secreted within the stone cat, the more bizarre it seemed, and I didn't want to keep the items any longer than I had to. The Nile far below my window looked tempting, but I couldn't very well just pitch them into the river, either. Clues of some kind, they might break up a drug ring, lead to the discovery of contraband arms, or uncover a repository for smuggled artifacts. Or, they could be red herrings or only part of a game. Whatever the case, the authorities would have to decide what to do, and Steve knew his way around Cairo much better than I. Perhaps he would go with me.

What to do about us I wasn't as sure. I would just have to hope that Aunt Miriam was right and that the solid foundation Steve and I already had to our friendship would suffice and that as best friends, we could work things out.

"Friendship with wings," she had called it. Yes, that perfectly described falling in love with one's best friend. It was time to be forthright about that with Steve, too.

Shades of before, however, Steve, who had always been as reliable about keeping appointments as the sun coming up, changed our lunch plans to an early dinner without explanation.

As it happened, although wild horses couldn't get me to the necropolis, Jeffrey could.

The knock on my hotel room door came when I was in the bathroom after lunch that afternoon. I called out that I would be just a moment. By the time I opened the door leading into the hallway, though, no one was there, and only a slightly bulging white envelope just beyond the sill gave proof that the knock hadn't been a figment of my imagination.

What now? I thought. I was so fed up with mysteriousness that I had half a mind to toss the envelope aside and wait to open it when I was with Steve. I wanted nothing more to do with Bastets, onionskins and a matter that concerned me only peripherally.

I placed the envelope on the desk and began a letter to Lauren, but after every few words I wrote, my eyes strayed back to the foreign matter. In the end, the envelope was a Pandora's box. It wouldn't hurt just to look, would it?

Carefully, I pulled the flap away and pulled out a sheet of paper.

Before I had had the chance to read its message or see who it was from, shock waves rippled through me as an enclosure fell onto the carpet at my feet.

As I picked it up, I was utterly stunned to see that it was a gold ring with a raised hieroglyphic inscription encircling it that matched the one back at home in my closet.

Jeffrey's ring!

Ignoring the written message for now, I focused entirely upon the piece of jewelry, slipping it onto my thumb, where it was still much too large, and remembered the last time I had seen it, on Jeffrey's finger at Sea-Tac as we had said goodbye before his departure for Istanbul. I had placed my hand over his and felt a current of exhilaration when I'd seen the loving symbol of two hands with matching wedding rings.

So much had happened since then.

Like a movie reel running amok at high speed, I saw my life play before me—the happily married image, the disbelief that Jeffrey was dead, the grief followed by feelings of betrayal, the move to Oregon, and the letting go. The reel played back and froze on the image of his face in happier times. I saw the way the dark eyes crinkled when he smiled, the gleam of his very white teeth in contrast to a skin tanned from golfing and traveling on business to sunny climes, and hair as black and shiny as jet. As darkly handsome as he was, he had been my Golden Boy, a man who could and would deliver all my dreams, a 24-karat person inside and out. A Golden Boy who had tarnished. I held the wedding ring firmly onto my thumb as I shakily opened the sheet of stationery. The typed message read:

Dear Lissa,

After what I've done to you, I don't expect you to be glad I'm alive. But I am. I've no right to ask a thing from you. The truth is, I desperately need your help.

Please meet me in the necropolis at the Church of Abu Sarga at 7:00 P.M. It's imperative that you bring no one, especially not Steve.

Please bring the cat.

I will explain everything in person.

As ever,

Jeffrey

Feeling weak with shock, I walked over to the window and did not see the Corniche el-Nil, the river, or Cairo Tower as, trance-like, I stared at nothing and rubbed the gold band that seemed to authenticate the missive.

I had to face the most important question of my life: Was Jeffrey—my *husband*—alive? Had the man in the camel photo, the man Lauren identified, indeed been he? Or was this a cruel joke and as absurd as giving me a Bastet with a key to a door in the necropolis was?

What would it mean if he were alive? Could he have been walking around with amnesia ever since the accident? Someone had sent me his watch and wallet, and there had been the description of the maple leaf birthmark on his corpse. Had my nearly cracking up been because I'd sensed that something was not right, that my husband might even be alive somewhere, somehow?

No, he had to be dead. Maybe I hadn't really known the man who was my husband, but I couldn't believe he could have stooped so low as to have staged his own *death*, made me a grieving *widow*, and begun a whole other life.

Yet here was his ring.

When I fumbled open my purse and took the camel picture out and scrutinized it once again, no matter how hard I tried to believe the figure in the background was not my husband, he looked just as Jeffrey always had.

All afternoon I agonized about whether or not to go to the necropolis.

I finally decided that I couldn't not go and perhaps wonder for the rest of my life if my husband were alive or dead.

Wisely or not, instead of meeting Steve for dinner, at 6:30 P.M., I was alighting from a cab that had just dropped me off on the fringe of the Coptic grave area.

CHAPTER EIGHTEEN

There may have been a better, more direct route to the Church of Abu Sarga, but I retraced the way Steve and I had gone what seemed like so long ago.

As I advanced into the necropolis, I wondered at what point I had ceased being a casual tourist savoring Egypt's panoply of history and local color to become a tool for . . . whatever this was. None of it made sense, but if the wedding ring counted for anything, Jeffrey—alive or not—fit in in some way.

I saw a motion ahead of me near the mourner's room with the ugly mustard-colored door, and my heart flip-flopped.

"Jeffrey?" I called. My voice sounded hollow.

There was no reply, and when I reached the gaudy portal, I saw no one.

Although the din of Cairo's traffic and teeming humanity provided a background noise of sorts, the necropolis was relatively, almost eerily, quiet, and empty as I penetrated into its depths. No tour groups were here now, no beggars that I could see, and only an occasional other living soul moved about this section of the City of the Dead. I knew it was foolhardy to be in such a deserted place alone, but something more potent than reason drove me.

I had to see Jeffrey—or not see him, as the case may be.

I had to find out for sure if he was alive, and if so, why he had left me and what he wanted from me now. Even though I realized that if it were not Jeffrey summoning me, I might be in physical danger, the need to know superseded caution.

The narrow dirt pathway lined with tomb after tomb on either side seemed like a morbid lesson in the art of perspective painting as I made my way along the route Steve and I had walked to the church. Oppressed as I was by the situation and the death symbols all around me, one elaborate tomb's peaked facade, flanked by a pair of marble angels towering over my head, suddenly caught my eye, and the heavenly beings seemed menacing in the filtered light of early evening, as if they might take wing and swoop into my hair.

A shiver ran through me, and I put on the cardigan I'd brought along.

"Jeffrey!" I called as I quickened my pace.

No answer rang out, nor did I see any movement around me.

I almost wished a mother asking for a handout for her children would walk by and target me for a few piastres.

Several minutes later, I saw the Church of Sitt Barbara and knew that Abu Sarga was just beyond. Now that I was so close to the appointed meeting spot, I felt weak with apprehension, which may be why the Bastet in my tote bag suddenly seemed very heavy.

As I transferred the bag from one clammy hand to another before hoisting it onto the opposite shoulder, I remembered the violent shove at Karnak when the other bag had been ripped off my shoulder. Whoever had taken it must know by now that it wasn't the sought-after item. Was I about to come face-to-face with this person?

As I drew even with the church, I wished fervently that Bastet II had been the right cat, because then I wouldn't be enmeshed in whatever strange drama this was—intrigue— that, if he really were alive, must involve Jeffrey.

If he really were alive . . .

How strange to be here now on the precarious verge of finding out if I was indeed a widow or still a wife. I had not really let myself consider what I would do if Jeffrey were alive, but the fact remained that I wasn't the same person I had been when we'd said goodbye at Sea-Taco,

I froze as a ghostly sound startled me.

"Over here, Lissa," I heard, and I felt as if I had stepped into another dimension as my ears identified the melodic voice I thought I would never hear again.

Alive! Jeffrey was alive!

The theoretical had become the actual, and *stunned* didn't begin to describe what I felt. It was pure *Twilight Zone*.

Struck momentarily mute, I finally found my voice and called, "Where are you, Jeffrey?"

When no answer came, I considered that perhaps I'd gone clear around the bend and imagined his voice. It made more sense, in an odd way, than my having really heard it.

Two Egyptian men strolled by. After they had passed, the voice came again, indicating that I was still sane after all.

"I'm here," he said.

My feeling of otherworldliness intensified as I saw the familiar form walk from around the Church of Sitt Barbara.

"I needed to be sure you were alone," he told me matter-of-factly.

I had always thought a moment seeming like forever was but a cliché, but we stood there, Jeffrey and I, rooted to our respective spots for what seemed to be the longest time.

Although I couldn't see his features well from this distance, he was unmistakably Jeffrey, and a kaleidoscopic whirl of clashing images *husband, stranger, husband, stranger*—formed and reformed in my mind almost in the blink of an eye.

As he stepped closer to me, I took a faltering couple of forward steps of my own and noticed that silver wings had tinged the temples I had once enjoyed massaging. I quickly pushed away the memory of the feel of his silky hair and its fresh lemony scent, but not before a moment of joy at having him living and breathing and in my presence coursed through me, only to disappear almost before it had come.

Suddenly, we were standing a mere three feet apart. "You're looking well," he told me.

Looking well? Why, he spoke as if we were only casual acquaintances meeting in the most mundane of circumstances!

I was so taken aback by his attitude that when he reached out an arm as if to touch me, I took a step backwards without consciously deciding to. Gone in an instant was the fantasy I'd had shortly after Jeffrey's *death*, when in my dreams I'd found him alive and we'd run through a field of wildflowers toward each other, arms outstretched and ready for the embrace of sweet reunion.

"You're alive. You're really alive, Jeffrey. I . . . I can't q-quite take this in," I stammered.

"I'm sorry it's such a shock," he told me as he glanced around nervously. "Let's move over there," he suggested, pointing to an area just off the main pathway.

Like a sleepwalker, I did as he requested, and then a silence ensued as we stood assessing each other. Except for the silvering hair, he looked as he always had, and I imagine that I did, too, though no doubt the shock of the situation had blanched my face. How ironic, I thought, that although we were closer in distance than we had been for over a year, a vast chasm yawned between us.

"Don't hate me," he said in a boyish way that used to melt me.

"I don't, Jeffrey," I replied, realizing that it was true.

Heartsick was more like it.

"I'm sorry I dragged you to the necropolis."

A sudden fury that shook me out of my trance overwhelmed me.

"Sorry for dragging me here! Sorry for dragging me here? Jeffrey, what about being sorry for the heartache you caused by disappearing?" I asked. "Do you have any idea what I've gone through? Do you care?"

He had hurt me so much! I longed for the remaining shards of my dreams to remain intact, but just looking at him, just hearing his casualness, was splintering them every which way. *Please*, I wanted to beg, *tell me you've had amnesia, tell me anything but that you walked out and abandoned me deliberately, like a cast-off shoe.* I didn't think he was acting like a recovered amnesiac, however, and I doubted even more that he had been held hostage somewhere. With a roil of nausea, I knew in my heart that he hadn't disappeared accidentally.

A shadow of something that might have been shame clouded the dark eyes that had once mesmerized me, and when he looked down at his feet, I almost felt sorry for him. Almost.

"What's going on?" I asked, surprised that my voice sounded so normal when my whole world had turned topsy-turvy.

Instead of answering my question, he maddeningly posed one of his own.

"Do you have the cat?"

I couldn't believe what I'd just heard. How he could just blithely ask for the Bastet without any kind of explanation or apology for his absence was so far beyond my idea of human decency that I was dumbfounded. Then a new wave of indignation crested.

"The cat!" I threw at him. "That's all you can ask? Jeffrey, where were you all this time? Why did you leave? How could you have left in the way you did? And don't tell me you had amnesia!"

His look of exasperation turned my anger up several degrees, and I had to fight the desire to walk close to him and pound and claw his chest raw for the pain he had inflicted. How could this man, this stranger who was my husband, stand there so casually?

"I didn't have amnesia," he confirmed with a sardonic smile.

"Why I left doesn't matter now."

"Doesn't matter? Do you really believe that? Maybe not to you it doesn't, but it matters to me."

"God, Lissa, what can I say? It ought to be obvious. The bottom line is that I'm a rat, isn't it? I walked out on you. Now, let me have the cat."

"The cat," I repeated, amazed that it all boiled down to being used.

"The Bastet, Lissa. Don't play dumb with me."

"They're for sale everywhere in Egypt. Why do you want this particular Bastet, Jeffrey? I rather like this one,"

I lied, "and would like to keep it."

"Come off it, Lissa. It's not yours to keep. Where is it?" he asked impatiently as I watched his eyes zoom in on the rounded tote bag. When I saw his look of relish, I felt sick to my stomach all over again.

Had I really thought I'd loved this man?

A vein in his temple pulsated as he demanded, "Hand it over. I don't have time for games."

"You don't have time for games!" I exploded.

This new, resurrected Jeffrey had a talent for pressing my buttons. Thinking of the terrible now-you-see-me, now-you-don't game he had played so heartlessly with me, I saw red. By some good fortune, I refrained from clobbering him with his precious stone cat and somehow forced myself to calm down. When I spoke again, my voice emerged with uncustomary iciness.

"Neither do I, Jeffrey. Tell me what's going on."

Our eyes met and held, and I watched as the wind seemed to die from his sails. Did pleasant memories flood his consciousness? Did he harbor any trace of love for me?

Whatever it was, he told me, "I could grab that carryall, you know, but you're right. I do owe you some kind of explanation.

"Shh!" he suddenly mouthed with a finger over his lips.

At first, I thought his spasm of wariness was only an act—a ploy to avoid being open with me just when he seemed on the verge of talking to me—but I spotted a darting motion just after he did and froze along with him.

After a time, he whispered, "It's not safe here. Come with me."

Although I certainly had no intention of obeying his every command, the element of danger, especially when the image of blood seeping through the brown suit fabric at Kom Ombo flashed to mind, was too real to ignore. I did what Jeffrey wanted.

Once we had found our new spot a little farther from the churches, he said, "I really will explain, but I need to see the Bastet right away. We're both in danger if we delay."

I made no resistance when he reached for the bag and pulled out the small statue that I'd begun to loathe. After unwrapping it and examining it carefully, he reached into his pocket for the penknife he always carried. His grandfather, I remembered, had carried it in World War II and given it to Jeffrey for his twelfth birthday shortly before he died. Funny, I thought, to recollect such a homey thing at such a time.

"It's no longer inside," I told him as I saw that he was about to pry the base away from the body of the cat.

"No?" he asked, looking up at me in surprise as his eyes narrowed. "Then where is it? What do you know about what's inside anyway?"

I explained how the cat had broken apart accidentally. "It looks intact," he said skeptically.

"I had it repaired without replacing its contents." A dark look crossed his face.

"The contents?' You don't even know it's a key," he scoffed as he undid the Luxor jeweler's repair job with his knife. Since he didn't mention the onionskin, I wondered if he knew what the key unlocked.

He was flustered when he found the empty space within the cat.

"Where is it? Do you have it?"

That's probably where I made my mistake. I should have just said no.

"Tell me why you left and I'll get it for you." I told him. Ready to say or do almost anything to get some answers.

Nettled, he said. "That's blackmail, Lissa. You've always been persistent haven't you, hon?"

"When necessary, Jeffrey."

And it seemed imperative now. If I simply handed it over and he did already know which door the key unlocked, would he get whatever he was after and vanish again, leaving me in a perpetual state of not knowing and a wife with a phantom as a husband? I couldn't take that chance. Deciding that he would get the key only for some information, I dug in my heels.

Familiar with my stubbornness about issues, like teaching, that really mattered to me, he told me, "Okay, you win. I know that look. But let me talk and don't interrupt. We ought to get out of here before dark."

He'd have to make it fast, then, because it was already getting dusky.

I listened then with incredulity as Jeffrey spun a tale of his travel writing having evolved into "a little artifact dealing," as he termed what sounded like smuggling to me. His legitimate business trips and active passport had, according to Jeffrey, made it easy, and he'd rationalized the smuggling by identifying with the private collectors who did, if selfishly, appreciate their acquisitions. The thrill of it had mounted for Jeffrey like an advancing illness, and gradually he had gotten deeper and deeper into illegal activities, until he decided to ditch his writing career and marriage to concentrate upon his new line of work.

I was struck as I listened by how the handsome external man clashed with the ugliness of what he was telling me, of what he had been doing and I realized more than ever that his physical appearance in tandem with an inner Jeffrey I had but created in my own mind, was what I had loved. In reality, Jeffrey Rohrer was as empty—as lacking in some vital inner treasure—as a plundered tomb. What forces, I wondered, had robbed him?

"Isn't there some way you could extricate yourself from this? You are an excellent writer, you know," I told him honestly.

Although he and I could never pick up where we'd left off when he had made the fateful decision to disappear and embrace a life of shady dealing, dropping out of my life in the process, I hoped very much that he could somehow abandon this way of life and find a semblance of inner substance.

"I've gotten in with some pretty influential people. It's too late for that," he told me, apparently resigned to the fate he had made for himself. I didn't believe it could be too late, but I let it ride. If he had convinced himself that it was too late, probably it was.

"Why involve me in all of this?" I asked. "And how did you even know I was in Egypt?"

"Believe me," he said with what might have been a touch of remorse, "I didn't want to, but everything started coming down on me just after I acquired the Bastet, and to protect it and myself while I decided what to do, I had to safely get rid of it fast. I knew it would be safe with you."

Which meant that I knew Jeffrey was alive only incidentally, only because I chanced to fit in with his new *career*.

I shook my head at the thought of his having put me in the midst of danger to protect his own skin.

"Jeffrey . . . "

"I need the key," he told me with urgency in his voice. "Someone is after the same thing I am, and I have to get to it first."

He didn't know me very well if he thought I would help him smuggle a . . . whatever it was. I wondered what it was this time. A fabulous piece of gold from an Egyptian tomb? A stash of drugs? A rare jewel? A Rembrandt? Treasure it must be for Jeffrey to have revealed himself to me.

"What's behind the door the key unlocks?" I couldn't resist asking.

"Something very special," he told me, and I saw his dreamy expression as he pictured the object of this strange treasure hunt with a certain tender admiration other people reserve only for their loved ones.

"It must be."

"It is, believe me. As beautiful as anything from Tut's tomb, and rarer. Carnelian, lapis, gold—a necklace worn by none other than Hatshepsut."

"Not the Allerton Collar?"

"Bingo!"

"I . . ."

"The key!" he demanded. "Now!"

Thinking about his *something special*, whether or not it was the legendary collar, had firmed up his drive to get to it.

"I don't have it with me," I lied even as I felt the key shift slightly within my bra.

I needed to try to buy time so that I could go to the authorities and let them retrieve the necklace from behind the carnelian colored door. If it was the Allerton Collar, it was a national treasure and far too priceless to pass into the hands of some greedy private buyer.

"Let's meet here at the same time tomorrow and I'll bring it."

"I'm waiting," he said, not falling for my ploy.

Jeffrey was losing his patience, and suddenly I wasn't so sure that I shouldn't be afraid of him. Although maybe it was a trick of the waning light, he had turned as menacing-looking as the marble angels along the path that had seemed poised to swoop down into my hair.

Yet I didn't fear Jeffrey, or even losing the Allerton Collar, as much at this point as I did the limbo to which he could so easily consign me by just disappearing again.

"You've put me in the middle of something dangerous, Jeffrey. Won't you at least tell me how you knew I was in Egypt?"

"I'm not sure you really want to know," he remarked.

"You're wrong. I do."

"Okay, okay, if we have to play 'Twenty Questions' to get anywhere, I'll play along. I learned you were here from Steve."

"Steve?" I asked dumbly, sick from the feeling that Jeffrey could stoop so low as to implicate his old golfing buddy, the man he knew to have been my longtime friend.

"You really look shocked, hon," he told me. "Don't you want to know where lover boy fits in?"

"He's not my lover."

"Doors, Lissa," he said as if I hadn't refuted him. "Who's the art historian fascinated with unique doors? Steve Matson. He's an important man in this operation. He's the one who finds the deserted rooms where we secrete the artifacts for a time, behind some of the prettiest doors you'd ever hope to see."

Was there a kernel of truth to what Jeffrey was telling me? I thought again about the same red door being in both Steve's folio *and* the Bastet, and I remembered his furtive examination of the statuette when he thought I wasn't looking. For me, though, that wasn't enough to go on.

"What . . ."

"Question and answer period is up, Lissa," he told me.

"What are you going to do?"

"1 said, no more questions. I don't want to get rough with you, but I will if I have to. The key!"

I knew he was determined, knew he could get it from me by force if he wanted to, and the almost maniacal fire that had lit his eyes strongly suggested that he'd use it. I was beaten and would just have to hope to get to the authorities before the collar left Egypt, which I was almost sure it would. I wouldn't do anybody any good if I were hurt.

"All right, Jeffrey," I told him as I reached into my cleavage for the old-fashioned key.

Wordlessly, I held it out to him. Just as he took it from my outstretched hand and I had begun to say something, I stopped in mid-sentence as a third figure approached out of nowhere. "Steve!" I exclaimed, never so glad to see anyone in my life. I took a step toward him.

But something was wrong. Not only did he not glance at me in reassurance, as I expected him to, he didn't seem a bit surprised to see Jeffrey alive.

It was his voice, though, that stopped me in my tracks. "Let me have that, Rohrer," he demanded as he reached for the key.

"Nothing doing," Jeffrey replied, slipping it into his pants pocket.

"No deal then," Steve said.

Stay away from the American professor with blond hair, returned Brown Suit's warning as it settled over me like a pall.

Then everything went black.

CHAPTER NINETEEN

When I came to, I was no longer outdoors, and the only break in the blackness around me came, dimly, through a small wrought iron window grille high above.

My first instinct was to get up and walk toward the fresh air and faint light that came through the latticework of the glassless aperture, but I realized with sudden horror when I sneezed three times in quick succession and automatically tried to bring my hand to my nose that my hands were bound behind my back.

A cord cut uncomfortably into my ankles and I had a splitting headache.

I thought for a moment that I must be in the middle of one of the troubling dreams I'd frequently had after Jeffrey's death. Then, as with nightmare ineffectiveness I tried to break free of my bonds, it all came thundering back.

The necropolis. Jeffrey alive. Steve involved in some way.

Where there might have been joy in finding a living husband, there were only bitter dregs of the keenest disappointment I had ever felt. My husband, the man I had chosen as a mate for life, was a—I couldn't think of a better word—a *crook*. He had been crooked in his secrecy when we were together in Bellevue, crooked in the way he had weaseled out of our marriage, and crooked in his way of life, especially now that it apparently included out-and-out illegalities.

He had had so little regard for me that not only had he let me suffer a widow's grief, but he had even propelled me into the midst of danger, using me as he had to carry around the Bastet, the key and the slip of onionskin with Steve's carnelian door on it.

Steve . . .

Wasn't it bad enough that I had unwittingly selected a crook as a husband? What about my best friend?

"The deal's off," Steve had said to Jeffrey right before I fainted. I burned to know what deal, what role in this strange drama Steve played, and to what extent he was involved with Jeffrey.

I found the idea that Steve could be involved in moving artifacts hard to swallow since he was an art historian who for almost as long as I had known him had held the conviction that rare art should be shared and appreciated by many people, not just a select few who could afford to purchase museum quality pieces on the black market and squirrel them away for their personal gloating.

The deal's off. I had definitely heard just those three ominous words.

I was amazed that, smuggling involvement or not, Steve had not seemed at all surprised to' see Jeffrey standing there alive. He knew Jeffrey lived! How could he not have told me?

Even though I still wore my sweater, I shivered in the

musty confines of . . . what? Where was I? The thought that I might be behind the carnelian door gave me the willies, and as I strained to loosen the ties securing my hands, though I'd not seen any in Egypt, I imagined rats or, heaven forbid, a cobra lurking in the darkness.

Work as I did, I only succeeded in rubbing my wrists raw. I counseled myself not to panic, but it was impossible not to feel it spiral when I couldn't ignore the tight restraints and wondered who would ever find me here. How stupid of me to have fallen into this trap.

I also wondered if whoever had brought me here had stripped this room of the treasure. That it could possibly be a collar worn in the fifteenth century B.C. by Queen Hatshepsut staggered me as I remembered the way her likeness had been obliterated time and again at the impressive Deir el-Bahri. I imagined that her personal effects had also been given short shrift by the regime of the stepson who had ruled after her death, with items like collars being dismantled and their jewels reprocessed into new pieces for the glory of the new pharaoh. If this were true, an intact collar that had belonged to Hatshepsut would be priceless.

That such a piece of jewelry could have stayed out of the hands of plunderers through the ages seemed unlikely, but what if an admirer of Hatshepsut's had hidden it well? The treasures from Tutankhamun's tomb, after all, had not been unearthed until 1922. In Greece and elsewhere, museum quality pieces were still turning up, sometimes by chance as, for instance, a street crew came upon an ancient statue.

Yes, the Allerton Collar might, indeed, be real, I told myself as I continued to inhale the dry mustiness of an atmosphere I could not see.

When a disembodied moan pierced the oppressive

stillness, all the mummy movies and other spook shows I had ever seen sprang to life, rolled into one horrific package. I had jumped at the sound and winced as rope burned my ankles, as well as my already irritated wrists, and set up a renewed throbbing in my head.

Cringing away from the direction of the sound, I asked, "Who's there?"

More moaning wafted my way.

"Please answer me," I called out again. "Who's there?" I heard my name said so weakly that I wasn't sure it had been real.

"Lissa," it came again, softly.

"Steve? Steve, is that you?"

"Oh, my head," he groaned, and I knew it was he.

"Your head? You're hurt!"

"Not badly," he replied as he tried to stifle the pain in his voice. "Never mind me. How are you?"

"I'm okay, Steve, but my hands and ankles are tied. I wish I could see you. How badly are you hurt?"

"I don't think it's serious, but it hurts like crazy, and I'm going to have a nasty goose egg, I'm sure," he told me as his voice gradually gained in strength.

"But that's wonderful!" I exclaimed, realizing that if Steve had a bump on the head, perhaps his only involvement had been following me to the City of the Dead.

"Wonderful? Hmmph."

"I'll explain later," I told him. Then I heard a scrabbling sound.

"Oh no! Rats!" I called out as I tried to make my body as small as possible. They might chew the rope securing my hands, thereby setting me free, but would they make my fingers their dinner in the process?

This time it was I who let out a moan.

"It's just me, Lissa," Steve, who knew my terror of rats, called out in reassurance. "I'm trying to scoot closer to you, but I'm also tied, and it's slow going."

I offered to meet him halfway, but he wanted me to sit tight.

"Where are we?" I asked to the accompaniment of the scratching sounds that were now sweet to me.

"In a mourner's room. After you passed out, I carried you here at Jeffrey's command. The gun he had spoke volumes."

Considering that hand pieces were staples of crime, it shouldn't have surprised me that Jeffrey had a gun, but it did, a little, because Jeffrey had, at least in that other life back in Bellevue, always been so opposed to handgun ownership in his own country.

"I'm shocked," I told him.

Then Steve was suddenly, wonderfully, at my side. Although in the darkness I could not see him more than as an outline, the way our shoulders touched was extraordinarily comforting.

"Are you really all right?" he asked.

"Yes. Except for a headache, I'm fine physically," I told him. He must know that the emotional toll was another story.

"Jeffrey tapped you on the head to keep you out, which may account for its achiness," he informed me. What a horrible moment that must have been for Steve.

"And you, Steve? Your head sounds in much worse shape than mine."

"Ha, ha," he quipped. "What else is new?"

"No, really," I told him, appreciating his humor even as I pushed for information.

It's bleeding again," he said.

"Oh no. I wish I could do something," I told him as I wondered if he had a dark splotch in his light-colored hair. I couldn't see him well enough in the dark to know.

"Let's just sit here quietly for a moment," he suggested, "and then we'll get to work on these ropes."

"I'm worried about your head."

"I don't think it's serious. It'll be okay if I stay still for a bit and the bleeding stops. I bumped it again on my trek from the other side of the room."

We lapsed into a brief silence.

"I can't believe Jeffrey is alive. Steve."

"You must be stunned out of your mind. I wish I could hold you."

"Me too," I answered with feeling as I leaned my head against his arm momentarily.

Then because I had to, I said, "You knew. Why didn't you tell me?"

"I would have, but I couldn't find you."

"Tell me what happened. How did you find Jeffrey?"

"When I decided to go to Turkey for more information about Jeffrey's supposed fatal accident," he began, "I never dreamed I'd put myself on the trail of a living man. I went to Istanbul for exactly the reason I told you: to give us peace of mind. But here we are, anything but at peace."

"I know, but you did find Jeffrey," I said, trying to lift his spirits a little. "Go on."

"Although the Turkish officials didn't much like my nosing around, one of them gave me the name and address of someone in Cairo—a man who had been in charge at the accident scene who might know more about it. I returned to Egypt and tracked down an Omar-something who, for money, was willing to talk to me about the accident.

"It turned out, Lissa, that Jeffrey, apparently wanting

to disappear, bribed Omar to identify the mangled body as his by describing, among other details, Jeffrey's distinctive birthmark. I don't quite know how Jeffrey managed all that."

"I can't imagine," I agreed, thinking how it had been mention of the maple leaf birthmark behind one knee that had clinched Jeffrey's death for me, ending my initial fantasy that the identification of the body as my husband's might be a mistake. Although it had bothered me not to have a body to bury, it seemed reasonable, considering the gory nature of the accident, not to have had the remains returned.

"Then what happened?" I asked.

"You and I had dinner, and although Omar's story indicated the likelihood that Jeffrey had faked his own death, I wasn't completely sure Omar was telling the truth. I wanted to follow up on one more lead before saying anything to you, because I couldn't imagine anything worse than getting your hopes up for nothing."

"So that's why you acted so weird last night," I remarked with sudden comprehension.

"I had just talked to Omar before meeting you, Lissa, and it seemed that Jeffrey might indeed be alive. It's one thing to be glad a man might turn up alive and entirely another if you've fallen in love with his wife."

Despite the grim setting, I felt something within me explode with relief and joy.

"You do love me then!"

"Of course I do. But let me tell you how I found Jeffrey, and then we can explore this other, much better topic."

"I'm listening," I told him as the need to know more reasserted itself.

"I didn't find out for sure about Jeffrey until this afternoon. I had the address of someone else who might shed some light onto the car-train crash. I drove there today and knocked on the door, and the most incredible thing happened."

"Jeffrey answered?" I asked, clued in by something in Steve's voice. When he murmured his assent, I added, "How amazing for you. You must have been shocked out of your shoes."

"Yes, but not as floored as you must have been. You always longed to find him alive, didn't you?"

"At first I did, but I had finally accepted it and moved beyond that. It's you I love, Steve."

"Oh, darling, you don't know how in love with you I am. Why, the joy I felt the day we went to Memphis knew no bounds until you thought of Jeffrey and . . ."

"You thought I was still in love with him?" I supplied. Now I understood so much.

"That's right."

"Still in love with Jeffrey? If only you knew! I was flooded with as much happiness as you were the evening we watched the sunset, but after so many years of platonic friendship, I was in a daze from what was happening and wasn't sure what you really wanted. I didn't know what I wanted myself. Influenced as I no doubt was by that camel picture, I also felt an intense sense of uneasiness connected somehow to Jeffrey, whom over the months since his disappearance I'd learned to know in a new, very disappointing way. It's what you sensed in me that went beyond grief. You might say I fell out of love with Jeffrey, if I was ever in love with him at all.

"Steve, I've loved you for years, but now I'm also *in love* with you, and there's just no comparison to what I felt for Jeffrey. It's the most beautiful feeling."

"Friendship with wings," he said with quiet joy in his voice.

"Aunt Miriam," I said. "You talked to her too?"

"Thank goodness you called her, because that's how I found out where you had gone." I heard his voice acquire a measure of sternness—I knew the hazel eyes would bore into mine if they could—as he added, "Why in blazes did you come here alone?"

I explained the note that might or might not have been from Jeffrey, the wedding ring, and my fear that if I didn't go to the necropolis alone, I might wonder forever if Jeffrey was alive or dead.

"I knew it was foolhardy to come here alone, but emotionally I just couldn't take the risk of *not* coming."

"I think I understand," he told me. Then, "Let's get to work on these ropes."

"First, what was your deal with Jeffrey, Steve?"

"When I demanded to know why he had left you, he admitted to running some minor league artifacts and stolen art from several countries for private collectors. You know how I abhor that sort of thing. Anyway, I offered him a deal—a deal I probably couldn't have enforced, but Jeffrey was a friend, Lissa, and I hoped I could jolt him out of what he was doing."

"Me too," I said, thinking of how I'd told him it wasn't too late to change.

"And the deal?"

"Either he quit cold turkey or I'd feel obligated to go to the authorities. Jeffrey said he'd gotten in too deeply to just quit and that he had something important to do before he could even consider it. He wouldn't specify, so I told him to take the deal or leave it. I never dreamed he'd arranged to meet you here or that you literally had the key to his latest acquisition."

"Minor league! Steve, he told me his current job has

to do with the— you won't believe this—the *Allerton Collar.*"

I heard Steve inhale deeply. "Then we've got to get out of here without further delay. Too many, a piece like that would be worth killing for."

"Is your head okay?"

"Yes, so let's start on the ropes," he told me, asking me to move so that we were sitting back-to-back. I couldn't reach his wrists, but I felt his fingers busily working at the rope securing mine.

"He couldn't get something that fabulous out of Egypt, could he?"

"I hope not, but I imagine there are ways, Lissa, especially via bribery." Frustration crept into his voice as he added, "Darn it, I can't seem to find the right piece of cord."

"Do you want me to try loosening yours? Maybe if I scrunch up a bit I could reach it."

"All right, but first give me a little longer with yours."

"Did he take the collar when he put us in here?" I asked. "He knocked me out with the butt of his gun or something heavy, but no, I don't think he took anything from this room. The collar, if it exists, must be behind the door Aunt Miriam told me about. The red door on the paper inside the Bastet."

"Behind the red door? But, Steve, I thought we were behind the carnelian door."

"No," he replied. "There. I think I've got the right section of cord now. It feels like it's beginning to loosen."

I had an awful thought just then and reflexively jerked my arms.

"Try to hold still," Steve told me.

"I'm sorry. Did you tell Jeffrey about the red door?"

"No, I didn't. I assumed that since he had the key from you, he also knew what it unlocked."

"He might have, but I don't think so, Steve. I didn't tell him, at any rate, and I didn't have the slip of onionskin with me."

"Jeffrey took the Bastet and your bag, as well as the key, no doubt thinking he'd find the missing clue inside. We've got to get out of here," he said urgently. "Jeffrey will be back."

Steve had just undone the first knot in the cord binding my hands together behind my back when the door to the mourner's room burst open.

The figure of a man was outlined against the almost hurting brightness of a flashlight.

Jeffrey was back.

"Where's the door, Lissa?" came a voice that, surprisingly, was not Jeffrey's.

"Richard!"

"That's right," he told me as he set the large flashlight onto the floor and, to my horror, pulled out a long-bladed knife.

"Don't touch her," Steve's voice warned. "Shut up, Matson."

Steve and I were shoulder-to-shoulder again, both facing Richard. As I felt the warmth of his body, I was sick to think that perhaps it was all going to end, almost before it had begun, just when we'd finally declared our love for each other.

Richard laughed at our predicament as he came at me with the knife, whose blade gleamed hypnotically in the stream of light. I felt so lightheaded. Was I going to faint again for only the second time in my life?

But when Richard reached me, he only cut my bonds and lifted me roughly to my feet, which had grown numb.

"Come," he ordered me.

"I can't walk," I told him as little pinpricks of pain shot through my wakening limbs.

"Let her go," Steve said. "I can take you to the door."

"No dice. You stay tied, buddy."

As Richard pulled me out into the night, I heard Steve call, "I love you!"

"And I love you!" I returned.

"Shut up," Richard told me. "One unnecessary move from you and your artist friend's hands won't ever hold a brush again.

"Now, take me to the door."

It was easier said than done. Other than in drawings, I had seen the actual door only once, and the necropolis was a maze now that night had fallen. It gave me a little leeway for stalling.

I started to ask where Jeffrey was, but Richard cut me off. "Not a peep!" he ordered.

His flashlight beam cut a slash into the night as we wound past dozens of tombs. If he hadn't needed me so vitally, I'm sure that Richard Calvin would have killed me on the spot out of sheer frustration as I led him first down one wrong turn, then down another. I sensed that I could stall for only so long, so using the tomb with the menacing-looking marble angels as my landmark, I finally did lead him to the carnelian door.

"There," I told him. "That's **it.**"

"The red one?" he asked as he thrust something cold into my hand. I realized it was the key. "Here, you open it."

"Jeffrey?" I chanced asking as I moved toward the door. "Is history," came the chilling reply.

Fingers shaking, I inserted the old-fashioned key into the lock and slowly turned it. There was a metallic sound. Richard's long arm reached out and opened the door. As he did, I thought about trying to make a run for it, but as if he had read my mind, his hand closed around one of my sore wrists like a vise.

"Step inside," he told me. "Would you like to see what you're going to die for?"

I made no reply.

Die for?

"There," he said, shining the beam onto a stack of crates.

"Inside each box are several soapstone cats, each with a hollow place cradling a piece of Hatshepsut' s collar."

So the Allerton Collar existed!

"Is there anything you'd like to say before I leave?" he asked me almost politely.

"Let the man in the other mourner's room go," I begged. "He doesn't know your identity and didn't see your face. The flashlight was blinding." Then, "You and Jeffrey were working together?"

"We were, but Jeffrey found out how fabulous this necklace is and decided it belongs to Egypt."

Hooray for you, Jeffrey! I thought.

"Jeffrey knew we were closing in on him and needed to get rid of the cat immediately. Since he knew from me that you were in Egypt, you must have sprung to his mind as a logical person to temporarily possess the statuette. His giving it to you and having a man follow you was his way of keeping control of the situation until he felt it was safe enough to act."

Richard had grown surprisingly expansive, so I risked a question: "Why didn't he just take the Bastet straight to the police?"

"For one thing, he didn't want to be arrested for past jobs. He also thought that the statuette was only a clue, not that it contained the map and key inside, too, though he learned that later. Jeffrey needed to know where the room would be this time, where the collar was, so he could remove any incriminating evidence *before* telling the world about the collar. Would you believe that fool felt a responsibility toward the buyer?"

I heard Richard laugh evilly and realized that Brown Suit's warning to *stay away from the American professor with blond hair* had applied to Richard, not to Steve. Richard's hair was darker than Steve's—a light brown really and not much of it—but to an Egyptian, Richard might indeed seem blond.

All the talking had suddenly ceased. Without taking his eyes off me, Richard placed the flashlight onto the floor and took a tube of some kind out of his pocket. As he screwed it onto his gun. I realized that it was a silencer.

Was this the end, then, or could I make a run for it? Looking around me quickly, I doubted it. The flashlight beam impaled me, and Richard was blocking the only exit from the little room.

He took a step toward me.

"Too bad it has to end this way, cutie," he told me as he aimed the gun at me.

I said a quick prayer.

At the same moment, I heard my name and saw a blur of motion in the doorway.

"Lissa!" Jeffrey called as he hurtled past Richard and flung his body in front of mine just as Richard pulled the trigger.

Suddenly, a much brighter light from outside flooded the room, and as Steve brought up the rear, men in uniforms swarmed in and subdued Richard.

Limp in my arms as I cradled him, Jeffrey took a shallow breath, exhaled, and died.

CHAPTER TWENTY

e took Jeffrey's body back to the Pacific Northwest with us and buried him quietly. Although Steve, Aunt Miriam and I said a prayer and read three of Jeffrey's favorite poems as he was laid to rest, we saw no need for a memorial service since one had been conducted a year ago. Nor did we feel that anyone needed to know that Jeffrey had willfully disappeared and strayed onto the shady side of the law.

Perhaps there is a hero and a villain in us all. In the end, Jeffrey had asserted the nobility of his human spirit, transcending the darker force which had driven him. Not only had he saved my life after freeing Steve and learning where I was, but he had drawn the line at helping to move the priceless necklace of an Egyptian queen who lived over 3,000 years ago.

The magnificent collar was authenticated and reassembled and remains in Egypt, where it belongs to the ages.

So many vacation friendships go the way of the wind, but the Brenners and I keep in touch, especially Lauren, who is a steadfast pen pal.

We also talk on the phone now and then to share the special events in our lives.

It was with something special to tell the little girl that I phoned her in St. Louis from my Oregon apartment a few months after Jeffrey's death.

After greeting each other, Lauren said, "Guess what?"

"What?"

"Daddy's taking me fishing at Lake of the Woods this summer.

That's in *Canada*, Lissa."

"That will be lots of fun. You'll be fishing for walleye, I take it?"

"And the big ugly ones, the northern," she told me, referring to another kind of pike.

"You will send me pictures, won't you, of you with your catch?"

"I sure will."

Then it was my turn. "Guess what?"

"What?" she asked.

"Steve and I are getting married in about two weeks."

"Hooray, hooray!" the little girl blasted into my eardrum.

"Have you told Grandma?"

"Not yet. You are the first person I've called."

"I am?" she asked, sounding pleased by her importance in my life.

"You are. I'm going to call your grandparents, too, but if you want to spill the beans before I do, that's okay with me."

"Are you wearing a white wedding gown?" she asked.

"No. It's going to be a very small, casual wedding, but I am going to wear a new dress, and do you know what I'm going to have on as my *something blue* Lauren?"

"No, what?"

"Your scarab."

"Oh good! Lissa, it will bring you good luck."

It might at that, but this marriage was going to succeed on far more than the whims of luck.

"Will you move back to Seattle?"

"Yes, and if I'm lucky, maybe I'll find a teaching position there or in one of the suburbs."

"Are you and Steve going to have babies?" came still another question.

"I hope so," I told her fervently, thinking that as much as I loved teaching, I wouldn't mind at all taking some time off for motherhood in the near future. I knew that I didn't want to wait too long, nor did Steve. It's funny how priorities change.

We chatted a bit about Lauren's piano lessons and puppy, and then it was time to hang up.

"You'll write me all about the wedding, won't you, Lissa?"

"You can count on it. I'll even send pictures, and I hope you'll meet Steve one day."

"Me too. Tell Steve *hi* and have a beautiful wedding."

"We will, sweetheart."

As I turned away from the phone, I told Steve, "Lauren is delighted for us and sends her regards."

"You two really struck up a good friendship, didn't you? I have a hunch that sooner or later we'll be driving to St. Louis."

"She'd adore you," I told him. He was so good with my niece.

"And I'd like her just as much. She appreciates *spooky* as much as we do," he remarked with a wink.

Even as we smiled, I think our thoughts simultaneously

flew back to the City of the Dead, where our experience had gone way beyond *spookiness*, into the realm of real terror.

"Lissa," he asked me now, "all that didn't spoil Egypt for you, did it?"

"Of course not," I told him, though I knew I'd never again want to set foot in Cairo's necropolis. Steve's book on Egyptian portals was in-publication, minus the beautiful drawing of the red door, which would always bring back that terrible night.

But that had been an outgrowth of human weakness and hardly a reflection of the land itself.

"I haven't stopped loving Egypt. After all," I told him, quoting his aunt, "'where else in the world can you see one of the seven wonders of the ancient world and hear the muezzin's call to prayer at the same time?'"

"Where else indeed? We'll go back," he promised.

"Next time, though, it would be fun to be just plain tourists," I commented.

"Definitely," he agreed. Then with a little laugh, he added, "Some hero I was, trussed up like a Thanksgiving turkey until Jeffrey freed me."

"Not all heroes rush in on white chargers," I told him as the warm depths of his hazel eyes confirmed that our friendship had finally soared unchecked. "You are my best friend extraordinaire, there for me on a steady, day-to-day basis, and that, my love, is my kind of hero."

THE END

ABOUT THE AUTHOR

Virginia M. Scott loved to write novels and poetry and corresponded with her friends around the world, long before email.

Virginia was born in San Francisco, CA. in 1945. Her adoptive parents, Dr. and Mrs. Charles Muhleman, returned to La Porte, Indiana when she was an infant.

At the age of fourteen, Virginia contracted meningitis and encephalitis causing the loss of hearing, serious balance problems, and epilepsy. In spite of her disabilities, she graduated from La Porte High School, received a BA degree with honors in English from Purdue North Central University, and completed a MA degree in Librarianship from the University of Washington. While at Purdue, Virginia won several writing contest and had her short stories published in *Portals*, a publication that included the winning stories.

In 1977 she married Dr. H. William Brelje, professor emeritus at Lewis and Clark College in Portland, Oregon. They lived in Lake Oswego, Oregon from 1977 until her death in 2001. Virginia used their trips to Europe and Egypt to gather information for her writing. She especially enjoyed France and the French language and visited there on many occasions. Her favorite trip was to Egypt in 1990.

She assisted her husband in the creation of *A History of the Washington School for the Deaf,* and helped him develop his book, *Global Perspectives on the Education of the Deaf in Select Countries* in 1999.

Virginia is survived by her husband Bill, a daughter, Amy, who lives in Encino, California and three grandchildren.

Her Young Adult novels dealing with overcoming the challenges of hearing loss include: *The Palace of the Princes* (1978), *Belonging* (1986), *Balancing Act* (1997) and *Finding Abby* (2000).

The Carnelian Door and *Don't Cross Your Heart, Katie Krieg,* were published posthumously in 2017 by her husband, H. William Brelje

CPSIA information can be obtained
at www.ICGtesting.com
Printed in the USA
FFHW02n0050211018
48819271-52987FF